SHOW ME YOUR HEART

By

Sharleen Johnson

Show Me Your Heart
ISBN #1-931742-80-4
Electronically published in 2002
by Treble Heart Books

Cover art is by my son, the photographer
Michael Wooten
www.memphiswootens.com

This book is dedicated to my husband, two brothers and critique
partners who offer their own unique expertise and who are a part of
every book I write.

SHOW ME YOUR HEART

Prologue

Thanksgiving Day

Memphis, Tennessee

Chelsea Hollander cautiously poked at the unidentifiable lumps of food on her plate. "What happened to Walter? I know he didn't cook this mess."

Claude frowned at his daughter. "Rena cooked it. I gave Walter the holiday off."

"The turkey is dry and tough," she replied as she shoved the plate away. "The dressing is soupy, totally inedible."

"I'm sick and tired of your constant insults," her father lashed out. "Rena is my wife and your stepmother. She deserves your respect."

The long formal table in the elegant dining room was too large for the four people seated around it. The multifaceted crystal chandelier fired a hail of twinkling lights against the wainscoting of richly gleaming mahogany. In the center of the white linen tablecloth, a tall arrangement of yellow chrysanthemums prevented Chelsea from making direct eye contact with her father, so she rose--so quickly the chair tipped over into the muffling nap of the thick carpet.

"I refuse to acknowledge someone five years younger

than I as a stepmother. Just look what she's done--moved in and started remodeling. She's packed away all Mother's beautiful things." Chelsea glared across the table at Rena Wheeler, her father's bride of six months. They argued from the moment the woman walked into the house.

"Redbush is her home. She can do as she pleases."

"She's nothing but a fortune hunter and you're too damned stubborn and senile to admit it." As Chelsea watched the color drain from his face, she was filled with immediate regret. Father and daughter were so much alike, not in looks, but both possessed volatile tempers. Lord knows, she loved her father, but he'd undergone a dramatic personality change since marrying Rena. Maybe if she had stayed in town after graduating from college, her father would not have fallen victim to that manipulating woman. She lifted her hand, ready to reach out to him until he stood up and met her challenge with a hostile expression.

"Apologize to her now," he demanded, taking advantage of her momentary silence.

Chelsea's temper flared again. "This situation doesn't deserve an apology. I was merely stating a fact. The food was poorly prepared."

"If you refuse to apologize, then get out." The threat in Claude's voice was strong and clearly spoken.

The flush of color drained from Chelsea's features. "What are you saying?"

"What I'm saying is…from this day forward, I have no daughter. You will no longer be welcome in this house."

"Daddy, I can't believe you're taking her side against me over a scrap of dry turkey."

"I said get out and don't come back until you can apologize." Claude sank into his chair as if the emotional confrontation drained him of his last ounce of energy.

"That'll be when hell freezes over." Chelsea switched her chilling gaze to Rena and asked in a sharp whisper, "Are you happy now? Isn't this what you wanted all along? To have my daddy all to yourself?"

Rena's chin jutted forward in silent defiance. Her greasy-haired brother, Sam Wheeler, appeared content to watch confidently from the sidelines.

Rena's smug expression caused Chelsea's loosely held temper to explode. She sidestepped the fallen chair, stormed from the dining room, snatched her purse and coat from the hall table, and hurried through the heavy oak door, leaving it open to the cold winter air. Her red Jaguar laid twenty feet of rubber skid marks as she gunned out the circular driveway. In her wake, the dry autumn leaves swirled in a riotous whirlwind of yellows, reds and browns, their colors enhanced by the last orange rays of sunset.

***

The thick smoky air was smothering as Chelsea stepped

5

inside the dimly lit nightclub. Raucous laughter erupted from a group of men watching a football game on the giant TV screen. She squinted into the darkness and saw an empty stool at the end of the bar.

As she moodily nursed a screwdriver, she relived the argument in graphic detail. Chelsea was well aware of her many unfortunate character traits: that she could travel from a wilted flower to raging bull in a heartbeat; and that in her twenty-six years, she'd never learned the knack of resolving a problem with soft-spoken diplomacy.

That's me! Explode first and ask questions later.

Although far from the truth, she preferred to think of herself as even-tempered; someone who needed to be prodded into anger. But on this awful night, disappointment and emotional pain combined to make her feel downright mean spirited. She was mad enough to kick something or somebody. Surprisingly, her fury was directed at Rena--not her father. The steel jaws of Rena's skillfully baited trap ensnared hotheaded Chelsea once again.

She stared into her drink and at the little pieces of orange pulp clinging to the sides of the glass. If she could turn back the clock and put a leash on her tongue, she might have handled the situation differently, but with Rena and Sam looking on, pride prevented her from saying, "I'm sorry." Now all she wanted was to sink into her father's arms and hear him say, "I love you, Pumpkin." How many times had she sought comfort in his ready embrace? He had always been there for her, but from now on, he wouldn't be. The unshed tears that gathered in her eyes were swiftly blinked away.

Chelsea was polishing off her second drink when the good-looking guy sitting at the opposite end of the bar arched an eyebrow and looked in her direction. The jukebox should be playing the honky-tonk song "Third-Rate Romance, Low-Rent Rendezvous," she mused as she acknowledged his quiet greeting with a nod and a fleeting smile.

He slowly and somewhat hesitantly approached and spoke with a husky, "Hi!"

"Hello," she responded with a throaty purr. She always felt ridiculous when trying to act sexy or seductive. But what the hell! Determined to set aside her misery, she pasted a fake smile on her face.

"Are you alone tonight?" he asked.

"Yes, my girl friend left early." She rationalized that one little white lie wouldn't hurt.

"May I buy you a drink?"

She nodded. "Sure. Another screwdriver will be fine." She promised herself to stop after four. Even then she would probably have to sleep for a few hours before being able to drive the ninety miles to her home in Jackson, Tennessee.

He paid for a pair of drinks, led her to a booth away from the boisterous crowd and slid in beside her. "You expecting sunshine tonight?"

Chelsea nervously fingered the cheap plastic frames. "I know these sunglasses look absurd, but the eye doctor dilated my eyes today." She winced at the telling of another lie, but felt the need to hide her distinctive violet eyes. People remembered the vivid color of her eyes even if they couldn't remember her name.

"Eye doctors are open for business on Thanksgiving Day?" He shrugged off her contrived response. "What's your name?"

"Would you believe Mary Smith?" When he burst out laughing, she peered into the smoky gloom to see if anyone were staring.

"Not for a minute. But I'll play your game. How do you do, Miss Smith? I'm John Doe. What's that tired old phrase about two ships passing in the night?"

"Yeah," she smiled weakly. "I like that old saying." As he looked at his watch, Chelsea noted that he wore no wedding band, only a large class ring from-- She angled her head to get a better look.

"I graduated from Vanderbilt University in Nashville," he stated, extending his hand so she could get an unobstructed view.

She blushed like a child caught stealing a cookie before dinner. "Sorry, I didn't mean to be nosy."

"I've got nothing to hide. I don't usually hang out in bars on holidays," he explained. "But my folks went to Europe, and I'm feeling sort of lonely. Hey, it's only seven. How about dinner and dancing? The Holiday Inn across the street has a nice restaurant and live music. It's Thanksgiving, we're both alone, so what do you say?"

"You're absolutely right," Chelsea agreed with a smile. "It's a holiday and we shouldn't spend it alone." John Doe slid out of the booth and lifted her with a gentle tug. His hands were warm and a little rough, as though he was used to physical labor.

The cool, crisp air of late November enveloped them with an invigorating blast as they emerged from the bar. The curbing presented an unexpected obstacle and she stumbled.

"Too much booze?" he asked as he grabbed her waist. His right hand remained in place, curled around the gentle slope of her hip

"Booze and these damnable high heels." *Not to mention dark sunglasses on a dark night,* she added silently.

Dinner went surprisingly well. They laughed about their experiences in college and the madness of spring breaks in Florida. He was easy to talk to, even though she was forced to tiptoe around the edges of the truth. Occasionally, he'd reach across the table and cover her hand with his; and the gesture made her feel cozy inside. Why couldn't her father have reached out to her this way? Was the cost to his pride any greater than the cost to hers? She studied her companion's hand, strong and sinewy, clean nails, and the edge of a gold watch peeked beneath his tweed sleeve. So like her father's hands.

Later, the sound of music lured Chelsea and her handsome escort to a small bar with a postage-stamp dance floor.

"Do you like to dance?" he asked.

"Love dancing."

He found her quiet smile was as beguiling as her satiny voice. "I'll bet you're an only child and your parents pushed you into lessons of every variety."

"Very observant. My father raised me. My mother died when I was young. At his insistence, I took swimming, dancing, tennis, horseback riding, fencing, three foreign languages, martial arts, piano, and singing. I failed miserably at singing."

"I can't imagine you failing at anything."

"Singing and getting along with my stepmother," she mumbled.

They found a table, ordered drinks, then maneuvered through the small crowd onto the hardwood floor. When he offered his open arms, she tucked the dark glasses into the pocket of her full skirt and stepped into the inviting circle. He drew her into his embrace and she laid her cheek against the nubby, tweed fabric of his sport coat. Each breath she took was an interesting mixture of soap, aftershave and virility. She was intensely aware of his strength, of his heat. She could feel puffs of his warm breath on her neck as he hummed the melody of familiar songs, and it created cascading shivers that toppled down her spine like spray from a bubbly waterfall. His hands were gently insistent as he guided her around the dance floor; and he seemed oblivious to his potent masculinity. Oddly, she felt safe with this stranger; the only sense of danger came from within.

As the curls of her silky black hair brushed his chin, he inhaled the exotic fragrance of expensive perfume, intriguing without being heavy. He surmised she was the product of a moneyed family, and yet there was a down-to-earthiness about her, a lack of the arrogance that often accompanies young women from privileged homes. His was a comfortable middle-class background, allowing him to easily bridge the gap between the very rich and the very poor.

Their bodies meshed as they moved in effortless unison to the strong beat of the drum. The loose-fitting sweater was hiding an abundance of feminine curves. He looked down at the young woman he held so intimately, hoping for a glimpse of her carefully guarded eyes.

They danced through an entire set until the three-piece band took a break. After they returned to the table, he excused himself. If she hadn't been too tipsy to drive, she might have bolted out the door. Instead, she put on her sunshades and drained her glass, welcoming the mind-numbing effects of the alcohol. The night, which began in fury and anguish over her father's traitorous actions, was ending quite differently. Now all she wanted was the solace of a pair of caring arms, a few whispered words of comfort

11

and to curl into a protective ball and lick the pain and freshness from her wounds.

John Doe returned sporting a quirky little grin. "Want another drink?"

She lifted her shoulders in a graceful shrug. "I don't want anything else."

Her fingers were laced around an empty glass. He grasped one hand, pressed a key into her palm and rolled her fingers into a fist. "How about room service?"

She couldn't help but respond to his smile as she met his hopeful gaze and nodded her affirmation. Maybe this is what Mary Smith came for.

***

The elevator was occupied, precluding the opportunity for small talk. As the metal box ascended with a hushed hum, her stomach plummeted. The doors opened onto a long hallway of muted lighting, sage carpeting and matching striped wallpaper. In her muddled mind, the effect was not much different than walking Stephen King's Green Mile as this tall stranger ushered her along with firm pressure against the small of her back.

John Doe unlocked the door, turned on the lights, then picked up the phone and ordered a bottle of champagne. Once she was inside, with the king-sized bed occupying the bulk of the room, fear began gnawing at her. She mentally sloshed through varying degrees of rationale to explain her startling out-of-character behavior. Men had degrading names for women who teased, then wouldn't follow through.

"You haven't done this before, have you?"

"Done what?" She feigned naiveté.

"Pick up a stranger for sex."

She wilted and a touch of humor played across her face. "In all honesty? I've never picked up anything more exciting than cat hair."

He walked to the closed door where she stood like a marble statue, and traced the line of her chin with a fingertip. "You're playing a dangerous game. There aren't many good guys."

She searched his face from behind the safety of her sunglasses, thinking he might be making fun of her. A couple of crinkled laugh lines bracketed the corners of his dark brown eyes, but she saw nothing hidden or mysterious. His intentions were loud and clear. In a brave and sensuous gesture, she raised her hand and lightly touched his cheek. "Are you one?" she asked in a timorous voice.

"Tell me tomorrow."

He brought her hand to his lips and kissed her palm, an action that generated a firestorm and sent its heat coursing through her body. Alternating waves of fire and chills swamped her. She tipped her face upward and their lips touched in a light, but intensely erotic kiss. More fireworks.

Startled by a sharp knock on the door, Chelsea pushed against his chest, springing free from his warm embrace.

"Room service," called a male voice.

She stepped over to the bed and sat stiffly on the edge with her knees clamped together and her full skirt tucked snugly around her legs.

John Doe signed for the champagne and waited for the cork to be popped. The door closed and he approached. "I hope you like the bubbly stuff," he said as he poured.

"For special occasions."

"Tonight is special. Can't you see tomorrow's headlines? 'John Doe met Mary Smith at the Holiday Inn last night . . . and the earth moved.'"

Chelsea was beginning to relax and enjoy his lighthearted banter. "We are sitting on the New Madrid earthquake fault," she responded jokingly.

He took the glass from her hand, placed it beside the bed and lifted her to her feet. When he removed her sunglasses, she dropped her gaze and leaned over to turn out the bedside lamp. Only the remote glow from the bathroom teased the edges of darkness.

"Not quite that earthshaking. But I promise you, my sweet little angel, I'll try to make it a very special night."

His whispered words launched another trainload of thrills. His hands skimmed across her back then pressed her body against

14

his. As she focused on the kaleidoscope of physical responses, her pain, hurt and anger diminished--not totally forgotten--but the emotions moved from the main highway in her mind onto a lesser-used side road. John Doe made her feel special, feel wanted, and for a while, overshadowed her father's betrayal.

When their lips met and his tongue invaded her mouth to taste her sweetness, the outside world ceased to exist.

Chapter 1

Thursday, Early June, Eighteen months later

Jackson, Tennessee

The final bell on the last day of school rang at three o'clock. The youngsters yelped with joy, gathered their books and scrambled from the classroom. This gorgeous day in early June was too beautiful for children to be cooped up inside. Even the teacher, Chelsea Hollander, was seized by a strong desire to get outside and enjoy the tantalizing warmth of the sunshine. The lure of summer vacation emptied the building quickly. She was retrieving her purse from the bottom drawer of her desk, when her friend Mandy peeked around the door.

"Chessie, you got a phone call in the office."

"Who'd be calling me here at school?" she wondered aloud.

Mandy fell in step with Chelsea; the staccato tap of her high heels echoed against concrete walls bedecked with childish crayon drawings. "When you finish, let's go to the Watering Hole. I was in Memphis last weekend and I want to share my juicy gossip."

"Have you got a new hunk?" Chelsea asked as they hurried down the hallway.

"Yes, oh yes," Mandy gushed. "And he's sooo handsome."

"And you're sooo shameless," Chelsea said jokingly.

"You change men as often as you change clothes. Are you always on the prowl?"

"As long as Amanda Foster has a breath in her body, she will be on the prowl. You don't get out often enough. Unless you've been keeping secrets from me, it's been over a year since you've been with a man."

Chelsea shushed her and cast a guilty glance over each shoulder looking for an accidental eavesdropper.

Mandy rushed on, "How can you hold out? I'd be frothing at the mouth if I hadn't had sex for that long. That's too much for a healthy woman like you."

"Yes, it is, but I've been busy with report cards," she stated with a sigh as she grappled to hold on to the dimming memory of that astounding night of passion eighteen months earlier.

What a night! What a man! She and her wonderful stranger had joined bodies like soul mates. Intuitively, he knew all the right moves, all the right words to whisper, when to be gentle and when to be rough. Even the innocent recollection caused tingling currents of pleasure to curl throughout her body. That oh-so-perfect lover turned her on like no one else before. These erotic thoughts pushed another sigh from her lips. Thoughts dominated all others, crowding out everything else. She kept those cherished memories parked on a private shelf in her mind, bringing them out occasionally to be relived and enjoyed. Enjoyed. Strange description for a night that began with the jolt of being disinherited by her father and ended in bed with a mysterious man.

Mandy ignored the faraway look that often claimed Chelsea's features and continued talking. "Every girl needs to get her cage rattled once in a while. There's something unique about having sex with a stranger--the excitement, the element of danger." She tucked a long strand of blonde hair behind her ear. "You can turn loose all your inhibitions--"

Inhibitions? Chelsea mused, allowing her mind to wander again--as if she had any control over her thoughts. *With him I had no inhibitions. Not a shred of embarrassment. Tasting, touching and investigating erogenous zones I didn't even know I had. I never felt so gloriously alive.*

"--knowing you'll never have to face the morning after."

"I didn't. I slipped away when the poor exhausted man fell sound asleep."

Chelsea tossed her a sweet toothy smile before disappearing into the principal's glass-enclosed office and placed the phone to her ear. Mandy watched with growing unease as the expression on Chelsea's face changed from pink-cheeked happiness to gray despair. By the time she hung up the phone, all the color had drained from her features. The expression on her face was one of absolute devastation.

Mandy rushed to her side and guided her to a chair before she collapsed. "What's wrong? What's happened?"

"That was, that was...oh God, Walter Scruggs." Chelsea's eyes appeared glazed and unfocused as she stared into space.

"Oh, yeah, the gray-haired Walter. The man who's been your father's retainer since the beginning of time."

"Oh Mandy! Oh God! He's dead."

Mandy sighed as relief replaced worry. From Chelsea's reactions, she was expecting far worse than the death of a servant. "I guess you'll be going to Walter's funeral."

"No, no, no. That was Walter on the phone. Daddy is dead."

"Your father? He's the one who's dead? Come on, I'm taking you home," Mandy insisted. "I'm not leaving you alone for a minute."

The house she lived in was the last place in the world Chelsea wanted to be. The walls and shelves were filled with too many photos and other mementoes of happier times before her mother died and before her father's remarriage. Too much of a painful reminder of the fatal tear in their relationship. "I, I need a very strong drink."

"Come on, I'll drive. We'll worry about your car tomorrow.

"Thirty minutes later, the two women paused in the doorway to wait for their eyes to adjust to the gloom. The Watering Hole was the social gathering place for all the young professionals who worked on the south side of the small town of

Jackson, Tennessee. However, the regulars didn't arrive until after five, so the room was empty.

"There's a booth in the corner." They placed their order and waited in awkward silence until their drinks were delivered. Mandy watched in astonishment as Chelsea drained the glass in three quick swallows. "Do you feeling like talking?"

Chelsea nodded. Her violet eyes were clouded with tears, sadness and confusion as her fingers fidgeted with the empty glass. "Daddy died. I, I just can't believe he's gone. I mean, I thought there would be a chance for us to, to--"

"To what? Make up?" Mandy finished the sentence.

Chelsea fought shock and numbness as she nodded again.

"Was it an accident? How did it happen?" Mandy asked.

"Drowned in the swimming pool." It sounded so much worse when she said it aloud. Chelsea placed her right hand over her heart, as if the pressure would ease the gripping pain in her chest. "I don't understand any of this."

"Slow down. What exactly did Walter say? Did he give you any description of how it happened?"

"He wouldn't tell me anything specific over the phone. He wants to see me in person." Chelsea refocused her eyes on her friend. "Mandy, he was whispering, as if he were afraid of being overhead. But he did say one thing--he doesn't think it was an accident."

"There are only two other options--either suicide or

murder."

"Daddy wasn't the type to kill himself."

"Okay, but who would want to murder him?"

"Walter didn't say her name, but I will. Rena Wheeler-- that woman he married." She couldn't force herself to say the name "Rena" and "Hollander" in the same sentence. Chelsea's tone was surprisingly venomous, as if for a moment, she'd lifted herself from the grasp of sadness. "She's the one who would profit the most from Daddy's death."

"Come on, get a grip. You can't accuse a person of murder after a two-minute phone call."

"It was the tone of his voice that got to me." Chelsea nervously combed her fingers through her short hair. "Maybe I'll wake up in a minute and find this is nothing but a bad dream."

Conversation paused while the waitress brought a second round of drinks. This was so typical of Chelsea, Mandy thought. She keeps everything bottled inside until she explodes like a hydrogen bomb--complete with the fallout of expletives. "What are you going to do?"

"I don't know. I don't know. I can't think straight."

"You better talk to your dad's lawyer, see about sorting through the legal hassles. What was his name?"

"Guthrie." A latent spark of pain kindled into flames. "There's nothing to sort. You know very well that Daddy disinherited me. Rena will get everything. Daddy was always a man of his word. If he made a threat, he followed through with it. He said 'You are no longer my daughter.' Daddy told me I couldn't come back until I apologized to Rena. My blasted ego felt the cost was too high." Chelsea's voice drifted into a near whisper. "If I could only take back time and unsay the words."

"You can't do anything about milk that was spilled eighteen months ago." Mandy understood her good friend very well, possibly better than Chelsea understood herself. They'd met in high school, attended the same college, graduated together, and now taught in the same elementary school.

After that infamous Thanksgiving Day argument, Chelsea admitted to Mandy that she'd gone to a bar and that hurt and humiliation forced her into the arms of a stranger. Her friend wasn't normally a promiscuous young woman, and Mandy secretly thought that Chelsea's night on the town was nothing more than an impulsive act. "Look, I know you've got a lot of animosity toward your dad, but you're the rightful heir--not his little witch of a wife."

Chelsea reflectively chewed on her bottom lip. "You know something ironic? I don't care about the money any more," she said, shoving the untouched drink aside, having lost interest in alcohol.

"Bite your tongue. You're not fooling me. You care. You were raised in luxury."

"Sure, I miss some of the tangible things that money can buy. But that's not the point. The point is...Daddy never tried to understand my point of view. Rena moved in and started redecorating everything in red velvet. God, it was awful. What makes men turn into fools over women?"

"You're sitting on it."

A halfhearted smile twitched the corner of her mouth. "Mandy, Mandy, what would I do without your humor? You keep my feet firmly planted in reality. You're the only one who stayed with me through 'richer-or-poorer.'"

"Hogwash! Poverty is not your cup of tea. It costs a fortune to live these days." Chelsea opened her mouth to object, but Mandy cut her off with a wave of her hand. "How many times have I heard that tired old 'I'm a survivor' story? Considering everything you've been through, I'll admit you bounced back quicker than I could have. Your dad canceled your insurance, your credit cards, repo'd your Jag, and cut off your monthly allowance, and then there's the matter of--"

Chelsea threw up her hand to halt the litany. "Yes, but Daddy couldn't touch my mother's trust fund. It's modest, but it keeps my head above water."

"Chelsea, you're the rightful heir to the Hollander estate. Why are you being so stubborn? Aren't you curious about what Walter wants to tell you? Aren't you going to your father's funeral?"

Chelsea closed her eyes and rubbed her temples. "I don't know. Lord, my head is pounding."

"Let's get down to basics. You're in denial. My mom and I went through this same thing when my dad died suddenly last year. What about the house, the furniture, all the family heirlooms? For crying out loud, that's better than letting some two-bit whore inherit everything."

Through the threat of tears, Chelsea mustered a meager smile. "Mandy, you are so eloquent."

"If Rena is as bad as you say, she'll probably have a garage sale and sell everything. Look, today was the last day of school. You need to see both Walter and Guthrie." Mandy grabbed Chelsea's wrist. "Listen to me! In all suspicious deaths, the coroner conducts an autopsy and an investigation into the circumstances surrounding the incident. Don't let 'what's-her-name' get away with anything. Jezuz, Chelsea! You can't stand by and do nothing. Get your butt to Memphis. I'll take care of things at the house."

***

By the time Chelsea made the ninety-minute drive to Memphis on Friday morning and found Tom Guthrie's new location, it was well past noon. Her father's old friend and family lawyer had moved into a different office building and she was forced to ask for directions because the workers hadn't painted the names on the door.

"I'm Chelsea Hollander," she announced to the secretary, too distracted to remember her name. "I'd like to see Tom Guthrie.

Is he in?"

Susan immediately recognized Claude Hollander's daughter by her distinctive violet eyes. Although her denim jumper and fresh-scrubbed face didn't match the image of the wealthy, well-dressed socialite she remembered from the past. Her hair was long and sleek back then; now her short black curls made her look much younger than her late twenties. "Yes ma'am, Miss Hollander, I remember you well. I'll tell Mister Guthrie you're here."

A few moments later, Tom limped down the hall toward her. "Chelsea, by damn, it's good to see you. I've been trying to track you down since yesterday morning."

"Tom, I've missed you," she mumbled in a trembling voice as they embraced with a long, warm bear hug. She experienced a wave of love for the old man who had always been a big part of her life. Even in the most dim of her memories, he was always there.

"You shouldn't have stayed away so long."

"Did Daddy tell you why?"

"No, Walter told me about the fight, secondhand information, of course. I think Rena was bragging."

"Dear old Walter. I've missed him as well."

Tom held her at arm's length and examined her. "You're looking grand, my dear. A little different somehow."

"It's called maturity, and I've added a couple of stubborn pounds. I haven't seen you in what--almost two years?"

"Since Claude married Rena."

Chelsea dipped her head and studied the pattern in the faded carpeting. "You don't have to remind me about that bitch!" she muttered vehemently. "Well, a helluva lot has happened since then."

"I see you still have your father's colorful language. You take after him in that respect. And you both have hot tempers, as I recall." Tom pointed her to his private office. "Go sit down, Chelsea, my dear. I'll join you in a moment." He stopped at Susan's desk and spoke softly. "Bring us two coffees with cream and sugar, and send Logan into my office as soon as he gets back from the courthouse." Tom returned and dropped heavily into his big leather chair. His broad smile faded. "Have you heard the news?"

"Yes. That's why I'm here. Walter called me yesterday afternoon just as school was letting out."

"I've been frantic to get in touch with you. Your phone number is unlisted and all I have is the number of your post office box. I was planning to hire a private detective and send him to Jackson to look for you."

"I made a deliberate effort not to be found." Chelsea scribbled her carefully guarded phone number and address on a piece of paper and handed it to Tom. "How did you hear?"

"Walter called me before I got out of bed yesterday morning. Said he was on his way to the big house to start breakfast, when he discovered your dad's body in the swimming

26

pool before six o'clock in the morning. Didn't know your dad was such an early riser. Anyway, I immediately phoned a friend of mine who's a homicide detective. He rushed to the scene to handle the investigation in person. Sweetheart, I'm so sorry about the senseless way he died. How are you coping?"

Chelsea's hands were knotted into fists as she grappled with the horrific image of her father having a heart attack or stroke and thrashing helplessly in the water. "Okay, I guess. I still have trouble believing this has happened." Chelsea looked up and peered into the old man's eyes. "Tom, how could Daddy have drowned? For Heaven's sake, he was an experienced scuba diver and an excellent swimmer."

"I know, I know. There are a few suspicions circulating. My new law partner went downtown to the courthouse early this morning to file a restraining order. We wanted to prevent Claude's widow from claiming the remains and cremating them until I could locate you. Legally, the widow is entitled to the body of her husband, but since Walter hinted at foul play...."

"Walter asked me to come to his place as soon as I could," Chelsea interrupted. "I drove by Redbush, but the main gate was chained and padlocked. He said he had important information to tell me. Tom, he could be in danger. I'm worried sick about him. Walter hinted that it wasn't an accident."

"He said the same thing to me. Let's give the man a call right now. Maybe we can go out there together. Rena has no grounds to bar our entry to the caretaker's cottage."

While Tom was dialing, the secretary delivered two cups of freshly brewed coffee. Chelsea sipped cautiously and made a purposeful effort to relax the tense muscles in her neck and shoulders. Yesterday's phone call from Walter was devastating. Claude Hollander, her father, was dead. The past twenty-four hours had extracted a heavy toll on her mind and heart, leaving her with the haunting specter of words that should have been said; actions she should have taken.

"No answer. I'll try again later."

"Tom, do you think Daddy was...was murdered?"

"Murder? That's a mighty strong word and it takes substantial evidence to prove."

"Yes, but--"

"Chelsea, my dear, it's not murder unless the coroner says it is. If he finds that Claude did not die of natural causes, then the burden of proof falls on the shoulders of the State Prosecutor. I promise you, every possible clue will be investigated. The Chief of Detectives for the entire City of Memphis is working the case. He's the top gun in the department."

"It has to be Rena," Chelsea stated vehemently, sidetracked by a rebirth of her anger. "She and that no-account brother of hers could have killed him for his insurance money. I assume Daddy rewrote his will."

"No, not through me. Claude hired another lawyer."

28

She was genuinely shocked and it registered on her face. "You two have been friends for over thirty years. He'd never do such a thing."

"Oh, but he did. Claude changed after he remarried. No more Sunday night card games. No Saturday mornings or Wednesday afternoon golf at the Country Club. I had to give up golf about a year ago because of my knee. But even before then he quit calling me--not a word, not even a Christmas card." Tom paused a moment to take a swallow of coffee, then offered a solicitous smile. "Chelsea, the will I have in my safe was written four years ago; and you are the major beneficiary. The only other bequest he made was to set up a small trust fund for Walter and his heirs. Regardless of his marriage, I simply can't believe that Claude would cut you off without a cent. You're his only child. He loved you beyond reason."

"Rena worked very hard to turn him against me."

"If Rena files a more recent will and you're disinherited, I hope you'll allow my firm to represent you to contest it."

"Tom, I don't want to turn this into a courtroom fiasco. That sort of trashy publicity could ruin my teaching career. Besides, I can't afford the kind of fees you charge."

He flipped his hand dismissively. "Cases like this are handled on contingency fee. Besides, we're like family."

"It isn't just me. There are other circumstances to be considered. I wouldn't fight simply for my own benefit, but I have another reason...." Unsure how to continue, Chelsea's explanation dribbled into silence and she rose from the chair to pace. Tom was old-fashioned in many respects and would probably be appalled by her indiscretion, but he had to know the truth. "I've got something to tell you, but I don't know where to start."

Tom hauled his bulk from the squeaking chair and adjusted his trousers. He was a big man, although not overweight, with only a few extra pounds stubbornly lodged around his middle. He leaned on the corner of the huge desk and massaged his painful arthritic knee. "Chelsea, I'm your godfather. You're the child Emily and I never had." He opened his arms to offer a hug. "What is it, sweetheart? You can tell me anything."

Nestled next to his fatherly chest, Chelsea found her lost courage. "Tom, I've got a son, Cody Hollander. He's ten months old." She stepped back to see his reaction. "And he's illegitimate," she stated bluntly.

Tom's eyelids fluttered rapidly for a few seconds, then he shrugged and managed to successfully pull off a noncommittal expression. "A sign of the times, I guess. Who's the father?"

"He doesn't know about the child. I want to raise my son without any interference. I've got no excuses and no one else deserves the blame except me. It was just a rare, impulsive fall from grace. Indiscretion is an appropriate description. A ridiculous attempt to get even with Daddy. So...here I am...Chelsea Hollander, single parent."

"When do I get to meet this precious little package?"

"Yesterday was the last day of school, so I'll have the summer free. I'll bring him to Memphis for a visit." Chelsea smiled and sat down again, feeling relieved that the truth was finally out in the open. Like all proud new mothers, she pulled a credit card case from her purse and unfolded a long string of photos. "Since Daddy is...is gone, you'll have to be his grandfather."

"Try to stop me." Tom chuckled over each photo. "What a handsome boy. Look at all that dark hair. Most babies are born bald as a cue ball. The boy looks vaguely familiar. Who did you say the father is?"

"I didn't, and I'm not." Chelsea studied Tom intently. "I don't want Daddy's money for myself. Only a small part of it for Cody, for his future, mostly his education. College costs so much these days, think of what it will cost eighteen years from now. You don't think I'm being mercenary, do you?"

"Where did you get such a ridiculous idea? This boy is a full-blooded Hollander. Your father would have wanted him to have every opportunity that his money can buy." Tom glanced toward the door. "I hear a familiar voice. I've been anxious for you to meet my new law partner. Wonderful man, just wonderful. I know you two will hit it off splendidly."

"When did you hire someone new?"

"About two years ago. Right after Jameson had the stroke, and with my bad knee. Plan to take on another this fall. That's why we're remodeling."

"Tom, you wanted to see me?"

The voice filled Chelsea's senses, overwhelming her with pure, undiluted terror.

Chapter 2

Friday afternoon

Memphis, Tennessee

Logan Wilder strode through the door of the law offices of Guthrie, Jameson & Wilder, and parked his briefcase on the front desk. "Good morning, Susan. What's all the activity?"

"Carpenters. Painters. We're also getting new carpet, new furniture and computers--we'll all be hooked together into one network. Everything will be torn up for another week or two."

"I've been so busy with the Baldwin case, I forgot all about it. Any calls?"

The aging secretary responded with an engaging smile as she handed him three slips of pink paper. He was just about the handsomest man she'd ever known. His dark, neatly trimmed hair was streaked with reddish gold highlights and his expressive, chocolate brown eyes were so penetrating. She labeled them bedroom eyes--velvet and sexy. A small cleft in his smooth-shaven chin added a whimsical touch to his normally stoic features. He stood tall, ramrod straight and was well muscled without being bulky. His perfectly tailored suit molded to the contours of his impressive body. After working with two old men for so many years, she found Logan an eye-pleasing addition to the firm.

"Mister Guthrie wants to see you. He has a client in his office."

"Any one I know?"

"I'm not sure. Did you ever meet Chelsea, Claude Hollander's daughter?"

"Never had the pleasure," he responded, then stepped down the hall.

A friendly expression flashed across Tom's features when Logan appeared at the door. "Tom, you wanted to see me?"

"Well, look who's here. Logan," he called. "Come in. I have a surprise. Logan Wilder, meet Chelsea Hollander."

The voice! Oh Lord, the voice! Chelsea's head slowly swiveled in the direction of the hall. It was him! The man she'd spent the night with. Cody's unwitting father. As tall and good-looking as the image squirreled away in her memory, his body nearly filled the doorway. The impact was powerful and hot, washing over her entire body leaving a residue of glistening pearls of sweat. Her mouth went cotton-dry and she felt dizzy and lightheaded. Panicked, she gripped the arms of the chair and pushed herself into a shaky standing position. The muscles in her legs were trembling so wildly, her knees threatened to collapse.

Logan was stunned as well. The ball of fire that ignited in his belly caused a faltering heartbeat. A momentary tightness stretched across his chest as he scanned her face with a critical eye. In the bright light of day, she was more beautiful than he remembered from their shadowy nighttime encounter. She possessed a natural beauty, devoid of masking make-up and shielding paint. She was the flesh and blood reincarnation of a fleeting but cherished dream. "Chelsea Hollander? You? You're Chelsea Hollander?"

"Y-yes, that's me." She smiled weakly as she stumbled toward Guthrie, snatched the stack of Cody's pictures out of the startled man's hands and hurriedly stuffed them into the pocket of her jumper. She performed the entire maneuver without taking her eyes from Logan's face.

"This is a jolt, albeit a pleasant one. But I couldn't be more delighted to find you again." Logan fought to regain his scattered composure as he moved closer. "I remember the face, but Chelsea isn't the name that came with it. If my memory serves me correctly, the little angel was wearing dark glasses on that cold November night, and introduced herself as Mary Smith. And that young woman was terribly rude and left the next morning without saying goodbye." He angled his forearm across his narrow waist and bent slightly. "Logan Wilder, alias John Doe, I'm pleased to met you." Humor tinged his voice.

Horrified by his clear reference to their previous meeting, Chelsea cut her gaze to Tom wondering if he had managed to calculate that two-plus-two equals one small child.

"Logan, what the hell is wrong with you? Have you lost your mind?" Tom returned to the chair behind his desk and massaged his knee again, grimacing with the fresh agony knifing through his joint. He was tired, in pain and extremely cranky.

35

"Please, I can't handle these little off-hand jokes of yours. Both of you sit down and listen. I've been to a bone surgeon to see about getting one of those newfangled metal knee replacements. My suffering is unbelievable--both leg bones grinding together with no cartilage as a cushion. The doctors have tried all the new procedures and nothing has worked." He tossed two prescription pain pills into his mouth and swallowed them with a swig of cooled coffee. "I can't concentrate on anything except the agony."

Recovering only slightly from the shock of the sudden face-to-face meeting with Logan, Chelsea continued to watch Tom as he raked his fingers through his thinning, gray hair. He appeared more frail than she first thought and his years seem suddenly to be weighing more heavily on his shoulders.

"After the surgery, I'll be out of the office for about four months going through rehab," Tom continued. "Logan, I've decided to give you the entire Hollander matter. There's going to be a royal battle. I've got a gut feeling that Rena has a new will tucked up her sleeve. I'll ask Susan to type the motion to name you Attorney of Record. I'm sure you'll agree, won't you, Chelsea?"

All she could manage was a slight nod. In all honesty, she had no one else to turn to. Logan released the button on his suit coat, parked on the corner of Tom's desk and made firm eye contact with the older man. "Hollander was your client for so long. Are you going to trust my judgment on this matter?"

"Logan, I hired you right out of law school on the advice

of my long time friend who was one of your professors. He told me that you had one of the best analytical minds he'd ever had the privilege of teaching. Every case Jameson and I have given you during the last two years, you've handled with finesse and expertise. I trust you to administer the Hollander matter as well."

Embarrassment over the expansive compliment made Logan drop his gaze to the floor. "Thank you, I've tried to live up to your expectations," he mumbled.

"Did you get the restraining order against Rena?" Tom asked.

Logan pulled a folded document from his inside coat pocket. "Signed, sealed and delivered to the coroner and the grieving widow, through her attorney, of course. Claude's body will be held at the morgue. There will be a formal hearing at ten o'clock on Monday morning to determine who's entitled to claim the remains."

"You'll need to be there for that, Chelsea," Tom added. "You understand that a body becomes chattel property at the moment of death, owned by the surviving spouse."

She nodded numbly, feeling emotionally battered. The implications of her father's death were slowly beginning to seep in. *Mandy was right.* She was mired in full-blown denial. Either unwilling or unable to accept the grimness of death. Her mother died of cancer when Chelsea was only thirteen. She was still haunted by the depth of her father's grief over his loss. Even now, as she grappled with losing her other parent, she still viewed death as something that happened in other families, not her own. Now, except for her infant son, she was alone.

"I assume you'll want to bury him next to your mother."

Chelsea nodded again. She tried without success to collect her thoughts enough to think about a casket and burial. As she fought the threat of tears, the secretary's voice came over the intercom.

"Mister Wilder, sorry to bother you, but your father's on line one. He says it's urgent."

Tom handed him the phone and watched intently as the conversation developed.

"Yes, I understand. Okay, Brew, thanks. I'll talk to you later." Logan replaced the handset. "The autopsy is scheduled for Monday morning. They're also going to run blood and urine toxicology tests to see if there were any illegal or controlled substances in his body."

"Excellent," Tom exclaimed. "As I mentioned to Chelsea, Claude showed signs of a personality change after his marriage. Especially confusion. We need that report to see if possibly he was ill or taking medication of some sort."

"Until that's completed," Logan explained. "We won't know if he drowned, or possibly had a seizure and was dead before he hit the water. It's fruitless to do any second-guessing. The medical examiner has to get inside the body and look around."

The sudden gasp from Chelsea captured the attention of both men. She wasn't crying, but Logan sensed that she was fighting mightily to keep her tears in check. "Are you okay?" he asked.

"Yes." *No, I'm not okay*, she thought silently. How could they speak in such cold, clinical terms? She wanted to scream, *That's my daddy you're talking about.* Chelsea was afraid of breaking into a flood of long overdue tears of sadness, frustration and guilt. She dipped her hand into her skirt pocket to grab a tissue and the photo case fell to the floor, scattering its contents.

Her eyes flew open in absolute horror. Cody's pictures were strewn across the carpeting. When she bent to scoop them together, she almost banged heads with Logan as he had leaned over as well.

She snatched the small case from his hand and stuffed it into her purse. "I, I've got to run."

Logan adroitly stepped in her way, barring her passage with an arm stretched across the doorway. "I'll need your home phone number. Tom said it's unlisted."

"I'm from out of town," she hedged.

"Where?"

"A couple of hours east of Memphis."

"Does this place have a name?"

He was standing so close she felt threatened, cornered like a wild animal, desperate to escape. "Jackson," she finally mumbled.

"What's your address?"

"I, I have a roommate."

"That's not an appropriate answer," Logan commented with a puzzled expression.

She ducked beneath his arm and retreated into the hall, but Logan followed. He placed his hand on her shoulder and applied light pressure. "Wait a minute. There are several important matters to discuss. You need to stay here in Memphis for at least a week--maybe more--so we can work together. The back-and-forth commute would kill several hours each day from Jackson."

Aggravated, she turned to face him squarely. "Mister Wilder, I may bear the Hollander name, but I have none of the Hollander money. I'm an underpaid, overworked school teacher and to be brutally honest, I can't afford the cost of a two-week stay in a motel." *Or the expense of twenty-four-hour childcare for Cody,* she almost added.

"May I be so bold as to offer you a place to stay?"

"I beg your pardon?" Her eyes registered shock.

"I live in a huge antebellum house that I'm renovating. It's got six bedrooms, three baths."

"I wouldn't dream of such an arrangement. I'll stay with Tom," she exclaimed and swirled on her heel, nearly crashing into the old man. "Oh, Tom. Do you mind if I stay with you for a few days while we're working on Daddy's estate?"

"Wish you could, sweetheart. But I sold that big old house about six months ago and moved into a small rented apartment. Almost every stick of furniture I own is in storage. Got no elbow room at all. It's this cursed knee. I can't climb stairs anymore. I'm looking for another house all on one floor, but haven't found one yet."

"Oh." Her shoulders sagged with disappointment.

Logan leaned his tall body against the doorframe and folded his arms across his chest. "So, how about it? My place?"

Logan's attitude infuriated her. "I'll think about it over the weekend."

"I promise to be a perfect gentleman. As I recall," he stated in a husky whisper loaded with sexual innuendoes. "I lived up to my promises once before. I promised to give you a memorable night...and I did."

Chelsea watched as Logan's gaze drifted lower to settle on her breasts. Embarrassment, mixed with fear of discovery, evolved into anger. "Men," she snapped, with the thought of Rena and her father looming heavily in her mind. "Big breasts turn your entire species into mush."

Totally mystified by the tone and content of their argument, Tom intervened. "Chelsea, Logan, quit this childish bickering. I can pay your motel bill, my dear, then charge it back to the estate. I'll have Susan make you a reservation at the Holiday Inn down the street a couple of blocks."

Heat seared the lining of her stomach. *The Holiday Inn? Lord no,* she anguished silently. As Chelsea's violet eyes slowly lifted to meet Logan's drilling gaze, she lingered on the sly smile that tilted the corners of his mouth.

"The Holiday Inn," Logan drawled. "By all means, their beds are very comfortable."

"You two run along and argue somewhere else." Tom continued as he herded them out of his office. "I'm going to try Walter's number again. Chelsea, I expect to see you here at nine on Monday morning. Young people," he muttered to himself as he returned to the comfort of his big leather chair. "These days you can't figure them out. Too much electronics, that's what I think. A push-button-world. Point and click. It puts a person out of touch with the realities of life."

Before Logan could respond, raised voices drifted down the carpeted hallway.

"No, I don't have no appointment an' I don't need one." The owner of a high-pitched voice was arguing with the secretary.

Rena Wheeler Hollander, dressed in a tight black dress and high heels, came hurrying down the hall. When she saw Chelsea, she stopped in her tracks.

"Well, if it isn't Miss Astor, the long-lost daughter. You must be here to get a chunk of Hollander money." The gold bracelets dangling on her arm jingled as she flicked at a stray lock of her dyed hair. "Well, I got a surprise for you, Missy. Your

42

daddy wrote a new will, an' your name ain't no where in it. Redbush an' everything in that house is mine, all mine."

Chelsea's old feelings for her former home emerged and blossomed. She battled the urge to snatch Rena by her long hair and beat her within an inch of her life. All the beautiful things that belonged to her mother rightfully should go to her, not Rena. The money was no longer an issue. Redbush was home. No matter how tenuous, it was the only remaining connection with her father and mother. That cauldron of emotion, an unhealthy combination of grief and fury, boiled over.

"You bitch!" Chelsea spit the words between tightly drawn lips. "I'll fight you tooth and nail." Her hand sprang out to grab a handful of hair, but Rena sidestepped.

"You stay away from me, you hear," she bellowed. "An' stay away from Redbush. Every lamp, every stick of furniture is mine, mine, mine. I'll make sure you don't get nothin'. Not one dish, not one red cent."

"You murdered him!   You tried to make it look like an accident. I won't let you get away with it." Chelsea's normally controlled voice gradually elevated into a high-pitched shrill.

"You can't find nothin', 'cause nothin' happened."

Sensing that Rena was about to start a brawl, Logan stepped between the two women. "Rena, what do you want?"

"From now on," she stated haughtily, blowing her whiskey-flavored breath in Logan's face. "You better call me

Missus Hollander. I want Claude's body so I can get him cremated. He wanted his ashes scattered in Florida." She waved the legal document under Logan's nose. "This paper says I can't have him."

"That's right. A restraining order is in effect."

"You can't do that 'cause I'm his wife."

"We can and we have. There will be a hearing Monday to determine who can claim the body."

"Well, Mister Smarty Pants, two can play at that game. I'll just go see my lawyer an' get one of them restrainin' orders put on the whole lot of you."

***

Rather than endure an agonizing wait for the elevator, Chelsea was so anxious to escape, she ran down two flights of stairs. Her car was stifling hot. She started the engine, turned on the air-conditioning and waited, her head tipped forward, propped on the steering wheel. Outrage prevented her from crying when her father ordered from the house. This was her opportunity, a justification to let the tears flow, but they wouldn't come. She was numb and dry-eyed, and yet engulfed by a profound sense of isolation and loneliness. She had no parents, no grandparents, no siblings, aunts, and no uncles or cousins. An aging lawyer and an elderly black servant were close, but they weren't family. Her wandering thoughts drifted home--the Redbush estate. The spacious rooms, the kitchen fragrant with the sweet yeasty aroma of baking bread, the flowers, azalea and dogwood. The lovely paintings, her mother's fine Italian china, the heavy teak wood furniture. What will happen to them now?

Cody, her precious ten-month-old son, was all she had left in the world. She was two months pregnant when she finally went to the doctor about her missed periods. Oddly, she experienced no panic or doubt when she learned about the unexpected pregnancy. It was not a child conceived of rape or regret, but resulting from a poignant coming together of two lonely human beings. She wanted the child to fill her aching emptiness and made the decision to have it alone. Maybe it was selfish reasoning, and equally selfish reasoning that prevented her from confronting Cody's father. Her faults were legendary, but whining to a strange man for support was not her style. The mistake was hers. Yes, it was a lonely ordeal, giving birth with only Mandy by her side. But by God, she did it--and without Logan Wilder. Now she had a darling son-- Cody Hollander. She'd managed to hold her life together alone, and was intensely proud of her accomplishments.

Living in separate cities was supposed to make it easier to avoid the man who fathered her child. She'd changed her phone to an unlisted number and began using a post office box for all her mail. Theoretically, there would be no way for their paths to cross. But being thrown figuratively into his lap slammed her into the stark reality of her decision to exclude him from Cody's life.

Her physical attraction to Logan was appalling--that

sweetly painful liquid heat. Neither time nor distance had diminished her reactions, and proud loud words spoken in defiance didn't lessen the effect. Today, her past rudely slapped her in the face.

She wanted justice, not romance. Gut instinct convinced her that Claude Hollander was murdered, even though she didn't have the facts to prove it--yet. Chelsea would find no rest or peace of mind until Rena and her brother were permanently behind bars.

The interior of the car began to cool. She fastened the seat belt and glanced at her reflection in the rear view mirror. She possessed her mother's violet eyes and her father's strong, determined chin. Unfortunately, she had not inherited either parent's level headedness.

Throughout her first thirteen years, two loving parents had nurtured her; during her teens, Claude had been both father and mother. Then there were separations, changes...college, teaching, his marriage and their breakup.

Pride goeth before the fall.

"I should have said I'm sorry. I should have said...damn, damn." She pounded the steering wheel with her fist to release her frustration.

Chelsea's secret hope was that there would always be a tomorrow--a day of reconciliation, a day of forgiveness, a day to forget the past, a day to introduce him to his grandson and begin life anew. From deep inside her private well of pain came the burning realization that there would be no tomorrow. Time had run out.

"Daddy, Daddy. Even though I never said the words, the Lord knows how much I loved you."

Chapter 3
Friday

After both Tom and Chelsea left his office, Logan stood by the window overlooking the parking lot and watched Chelsea emerge from the building, hurry toward her nondescript little white Chevy and get in. The distance was too great to read her license tag. Heat radiated from the black asphalt surface creating wavy apparitions. In silhouette, it appeared she bent her head over the steering wheel and remained still for a long time. Too long. He imagined that she was crying. The face she presented to others was too controlled; too composed for the tragedy she had endured. As soon as Chelsea fled, Tom filled him in on some of the circumstances surrounding the break-up between father and daughter. Logan ventured a secure guess that Chelsea was consumed by guilt over the hostile split with her father and that he'd died before she could arrange a reconciliation.

"She is a very proud young woman," he mused quietly. "Too proud to vent her sorrow in public, but too angry to contain her rage." He continued to watch as she beat on the steering wheel, then drove away.

He took off his suit jacket and carefully hung it up. If Tom was going to trust him to handle the case as he wanted, then that's just what he was going to do. He sat down at his desk and quickly dialed his father. "Brew, can you get me the police report

48

for the night Claude Hollander died? Yes, I'd like to know how the crime scene was handled, tests done, copies of statements. You know what I need. What's your personal, off-the-record opinion? Do you think Claude Hollander was murdered?" Logan listened for several minutes. "That's great, Dad. Yes, no, maybe. You're a pillar of indecision. We'll all know for certain by Tuesday."

After ending the short conversation, Logan leaned back in his chair and stared at the ceiling. Why did Chelsea make such a fuss over giving out her phone number and address? Certainly nothing earth shattering. Why the mystery?

"Chelsea Hollander." He stroked his fingers over the sharp line of his jaw as he muttered her name aloud. "I feel like you're afraid of me, but I can't figure out why." Tom tapped on the opened door and distracted him from his daydreams. "What's up, Tom?"

"I just wanted to emphasize my faith in your legal qualifications. You seem unsure of your ability to direct the Hollander matter. I don't understand your reluctance."

"I know, but I've only handled civil cases and some white-collar crime, not criminal investigations. We could be talking about something as serious as murder."

"The District Attorney's office will prosecute if there's enough evidence. Besides, it'll be good experience for you. Widen your horizons." Tom dipped into his shirt pocket and handed Logan a stack of dog-eared photos. "I was going through some old pictures in my desk drawer and found these of Chelsea and the family. She's a stunning girl. Watched her grow up. Spunky little lady, standing toe to toe with Rena like she did. Colorful language, just like her dad. What a tomboy. Always trailing after Claude at his construction sites wearing heavy boots and a yellow hard hat. What a sight."

What a sight indeed. But the picture haunting Logan's mind was radically different than the one with her sitting on the hood of a red Jaguar festooned with Christmas ribbons. The image he held most dearly was of her wearing nothing at all...except a string of pearls nestled against the warm flesh of her neck. She was all curves, shadows and golden perfection.

"That's Emily in the chair and Claude by the swimming pool," Tom pointed. "Hollander wasn't a millionaire when he walked into the office of a struggling young attorney thirty-three years ago."

"Hard to visualize you as young and struggling," Logan stated with a lopsided smile.

"So much has happened since those days. Claude wanted her to study engineering and architecture, take over the family construction business," Tom continued to ramble. "But she had her heart set on becoming a teacher, always loved kids. You know, she's part Cherokee on her paternal side. That's where she gets all that black hair and beautiful complexion. Some distant great-grandmother came out of the hill country in northern Alabama.

Chelsea's mother was Italian--Donati. The girl is definitely a unique combination." Tom tossed the photos on Logan's desk before he collapsed in the chair and absentmindedly rubbed his sore knee. "We used to have so much fun at Redbush on holidays-- swim parties, barbecues, formal dinners. Ever since Emily died, life is no fun. In fact, holidays are miserable now. What did you do last weekend?"

"Memorial Day? I went to a cookout with my brother, his wife and a couple of rough-and-tumble nephews. Then I did some more work on my house."

"It's a bitch growing old alone--excuse my language. Claude might not have remarried if Chelsea had stayed here in Memphis. Since Emily died, can't say I ever got lonely enough or desperate enough to marry a...You know what I mean?"

"Not really." Logan baited the old man for the fun of it.

"A woman with a jaded past."

Logan laughed softly. "You might think about buying a dog or a cat."

"No jokes, Logan. You need to get married, start a family. Time has a way of creeping up on a man."

"Sure. I'll go out next week and find myself a little woman." He offered an affectionate smile to the older man. Tom delivered the same stern warning before every holiday throughout the calendar year.

Seventeen Eleven Central Avenue was located in the old "Garden District" of Memphis. The place had been suffering from neglect when he'd bought it the previous year at a tax auction. Since then, he'd devoted every moment of his free time doing the renovations. Some guys liked to tinker with old cars; his passion was old houses, and bringing dull old wood back to its lustrous glory.

The house was dark and uninviting as he straggled in the back door with his heavy briefcase. Tom was right, it's damned lonely coming home to an empty house. He might even consider getting a dog. Something large and friendly--like a Black Lab or Golden Retriever. It was easy to commiserate with the men who sought the convivial atmosphere of a neighborhood bar. There were times when he was sorely tempted. He peered into the freezer. Not much to choose from, but he wasn't in the mood to go out. He selected an unappetizing TV dinner, popped it into the microwave and sorted through the stack of mail while he waited.

For some strange reason, he'd pocketed the two snapshots of Chelsea that Tom had casually tossed on his desk. He put them on the refrigerator door, holding them in place with a magnet--a gift from one of his nephews stating, "To a Super Uncle."

No matter how hard he tried to divert his attention, Logan was hypnotized by the fascinating face smiling back at him. There was spontaneity about her, as if her lips were poised to say something cutting or witty. In one photo, she was wearing a body-hugging swimsuit, standing by the pool with Claude, Tom and Emily in the background.

The top was cut low to reveal her deeply shadowed cleavage and the enticing swell of breasts so tantalizing he wanted to reach out and touch their silky softness. The lady was indeed well endowed. Those Liz Taylor eyes were extraordinary, a vivid shade of violet with a golden spark of intelligence glistening brightly in their depths. Now he could understand why, on the night they met, she wore dark glasses to hide her distinctive eyes. Their radiance and richness of color would have been as impossible to forget then as they are now. Maybe it was their disguised identities that had escalated passion to new and dizzying heights. Or maybe theirs was that proverbial match-made-in-Heaven; an encounter ordained by Fate, not by chance. Whatever. Her uniqueness was the treasured memory he had clung to for nearly two years. How could Chelsea unknowingly insinuate herself into his well-ordered life after only one meeting? It was puzzling.

These days his life was becoming a little too well ordered. By no stretch of the imagination could anyone call him a loner, but at the moment, there was no one special in his life. The few women he dated were dedicated professionals like himself only looking for a little temporary satisfaction while they attempted to climb the shaky ladder of success. That's all he could handle right now while he was attempting to negotiate that same unstable ladder.

He wasn't an unhappy man, simply too busy with his law career to indulge in a serious relationship. Work, work and more work. A single-minded determination to become the best-damned lawyer in the city of Memphis. His court cases were researched in excruciating detail, spending long hours in the law library or at his home computer scanning digital libraries accessed through the Internet. Yes, on occasion, loneliness had driven him to haunt the night scene looking for that elusive "Miss Right." Apparently, the ideal woman existed only in his mind. There were two notable exceptions; one moved in with him, "For one very long month," he said aloud.

The other notable exception was, until today, little more than a fading memory. A handful of recollections of a nameless young woman who drifted into his life for one incredible night of lovemaking, then vanished without a trace, an angel that had fallen from heaven, then flown away. Why had he not had a clear moment of peace since then? He would wake up in the night, sleepily reach out, only to have the illusion dissolve under the harsh scrutiny of reality.

During the intervening months, he had occasionally succumbed to a strictly physical urge. But he'd always come away with a strange restlessness, castigating himself for giving in to meaningless, gratuitous sex.

He wiped an imaginary fingerprint from the photo. "Now I can give that face a name."

Hindsight was being exceptionally cruel. He knew that it was in bad taste to have brought up the fact in front of Tom that they had spent the night together. However, his shock at seeing her knocked him for a loop, at least momentarily. But, was that what was behind her reaction to him? Fear that Tom would learn about her indiscretion? Just because they'd spent an intimate night together didn't mean it would interfere with their business relationship. Was that a reason to fear him? Embarrassed, maybe, but why fear?

Of course, if she could have read my mind.... He chuckled aloud.

With more of the illuminating benefits of hindsight, Logan could better understand Chelsea's behavior the night they first met. The feelings of betrayal and abandonment by her father made her reach for the temporary comfort of the bottle, then for the more physical comfort she found in his arms. He shivered slightly as a wave of sexual arousal flowed over his body.

The microwave beeped and he removed the steaming tray.

Chapter 4

Friday evening

Jackson, Tennessee

Chelsea drove home to Jackson at breakneck speed, cruising along I-40 while fiercely battling her conscience. Seeing Logan activated too many remote memories, as if she could ever force herself to forget them. As the heat suffused her body, she bumped the air-conditioning up a notch. No man had ever built such a roaring fire in her. Oddly errant thoughts crept in.

When in her late teens and early twenties, Chelsea thought there might be something physically wrong with her. After hearing Mandy's eloquent descriptions of hot need and passionate responses, she wondered why she hadn't experienced the same feelings. Then along came Logan. Chelsea shook her head and gripped the steering wheel tighter. She desperately wanted to be rid of these pesky reflections, and to forget that night. But how could she? Every time Cody looked up at her with those liquid dark brown eyes, she could see the boy's likeness to his father reflected there.

Lord knows, she was being jerked in a dozen different directions. *Daddy. Daddy.* She was engulfed by grief...because he was gone. Guilt...that she hadn't made an attempt to mend their relationship. Rage...because he might have been murdered. Shock...at meeting Logan. Fear...that he might find out about

Cody. One more emotion was begging for recognition. Dare she give it a name?

***

The clock was chiming six as she walked into the house. She ignored the purred greeting from Katie-the-cat, snatched the cordless phone from its base and tapped out Mandy's number. "Mandy, Mandy, it's me."

"Hey, how'd it go in Memphis?"

"You won't believe it. It's him. What am I going to do?"

"Slow down. What are you babbling about? Who is him?"

"A year and a half ago. You know, my one-night-stand," Chelsea ranted as she paced the floor. "Don't you remember? Cody's father."

"I don't know what you're raving about. You're talking too fast. Slow down."

"Bring Cody home from your mom's, would you? I've just got to talk to someone or I'll bust wide open."

"Okay. Give me half an hour. I'll stop for a pizza."

Chelsea continued to stride the length of the living room until she heard the distinctive rattle of Mandy's old car. She fumbled with the chain and yanked open the door. Mandy was balancing Cody in one arm and the pizza in the other.

"Thank goodness, you're here. I'm about to explode."

"You're always ready to explode. Please, go slow. Settle

down and begin at the beginning. Don't confuse me."

Chelsea scooped Cody into her arms, nuzzling him, mumbling baby talk, reveling in his unique baby aromas. He squealed with delight and grabbed a handful of her hair and tried to stuff it into his mouth. "Oh, my big baby boy must be hungry. Come on, let's go in the kitchen. I followed your advice and went to see Tom Guthrie today." Chelsea tossed the words over her shoulder as she led the way. "We tried to get in touch with Walter, but he's not answering his phone. Either that or he's gone, or, or worse."

"What's this got to do with the guy you shacked up with two years ago?"

"Eighteen months to be exact. I ran smack into Cody's father. If his name had been on the door, I'd have run for my life. Oh my lord, what if he saw Cody's carseat."

"I thought you didn't know his name."

"It was my secret."

Mandy scowled and put her hands on her hips. "Well, this is a fine kettle of fish. It's the first time you've lied to me since we first met. I thought we shared all our little secrets."

"Please try to understand. Desperate situations require desperate actions. When I learned I was pregnant, I went to the library and found him in the Vanderbilt College Yearbook. I didn't notice his career choice. Knowing his name seemed dangerous enough. Thank goodness I didn't tell him where I went to college."

"All those years of friendship," Mandy muttered dejectedly. "Down the drain."

"Nothing is wrong with our friendship. You're overreacting." Chelsea placed her hand on Mandy's shoulder. "Look, I'm sorry, but I was afraid that you'd take it upon yourself to tell him."

"I won't lie and say the thought didn't cross my mind."

"Maybe I've been wrong."

"I've preached that from the very beginning."

"I know, but I didn't want the hassle of some stranger fighting me for visitation rights." Chelsea put Cody in his high chair and tied a large bib around his neck. He was drooling and ogling the fragrant pizza. "No you don't, little man. You'll get a tummy ache. Here's your binky. Mandy, you won't believe this, but Logan Wilder is a law partner with Guthrie."

"I thought there was another old guy."

"Yes, Will Jameson, but he's recovering from a stroke, and Guthrie is in poor health as well, so he hired another lawyer. Logan Wilder has taken over most of the case load for the firm."

"Are you sure he's the same man? That's stretching coincidence to the outer limits."

"It's him all right."

"You know, you were a whole bunch mad and a little bit drunk that night"

"Yes, and I had a humdinger of a headache the next day."

She grimaced with the memory. "That's what I get for choosing a bar too close to Tom's old office."

"Maybe he forgot. Did he mention having an intimate little rendezvous with you?"

"You bet he did, and joyfully. In fact, the way he kept referring to our November encounter, I was afraid Tom would figured out that Logan was Cody's father."

"You told Tom about Cody?"

"Yes, I wanted him to know why I wanted a piece of Daddy's money. College tuition and such. That's all. Nothing for me. Poor Tom, he's so distracted by his knee pain, he didn't make the connection."

Mandy set the kitchen table for their meal of pizza while Chelsea heated Cody's baby food in the microwave. He was impatiently banging his spoon on the tray of his high chair, accompanied by his high-pitched chatter, so Chelsea gave him a cracker to nibble on. Katie-the-cat was perched beneath Cody, waiting for the inevitable fall-out of crumbs.

"Tell me more about Logan," Mandy insisted.

"I'm sure I was one of many midnight encounters Logan Wilder has had. I'll bet he has an ego the size of Mount Rushmore."

"That handsome?" Mandy asked.

"It should be against the law for a man to be that good looking."

"You're not chopped liver."

"Look at me! I'm too short; my feet too small; my legs too long; my breasts too large. Nothing matches."

"He probably didn't look higher than those cantaloupes you carry around. You've never gotten around to giving me all the juicy and delicious details. That must have been some night."

"It was," Chelsea mused, allowing her mind to wander once again.

"I see that faraway look in your eyes. Come on back to planet earth, Chessie."

"Something very strange was going on with Daddy. After our breakup, he hired a different lawyer and according to Tom, was acting confused. Quit calling, quit playing golf. That's bizarre behavior because Daddy always lived by routine--golf on Wednesday afternoon and Saturday morning, Sunday dinner at the country club. Rena is probably behind all the changes of people and routines. If she files a newer will that disinherits me, then Logan will represent me to contest it. He and I will have to work together on this case." Chelsea paused and faced Mandy. "Logan wants me to stay at his place in Memphis."

"In his house? Are you going?"

"Yes. No," she stated emphatically. "I'm so rattled."

"I can see that."

"Yes, I'm going to Memphis, but I'll be staying at the same Holiday Inn where we--"

"This is getting very interesting." Mandy smiled gleefully as she tucked a lock of blonde hair behind her ear and peered into the refrigerator. "Got any beer? Wine doesn't go with pizza."

"The make-believe stuff. Bottom shelf."

"Damn, non-alcoholic," Mandy muttered.

"I can't let him come to Jackson looking for me. He might see Cody."

"My mom can take care of Cody, but it looks like you're caught between a rock and a hard place. How long will you have to stay there?" Mandy asked.

"I don't know. A week, maybe two. There's a court hearing on Monday to determine who gets Daddy's body, and there's going to be an investigation into Daddy's death."

"He was murdered?"

"I'm betting he was. Walter sounded so scared on the phone, although he didn't actually say the words. Now the poor old man has disappeared. There's also going to be a court hearing Monday to settle who gets Daddy's body. Monday's going to be busy as they'll do the autopsy. I guess the coroner has the final say-so. If it was murder, the investigation will continue. If not, well, I don't know what will happen."

"That's right, that's the law. My dad died of a heart attack in his office, but it was treated like a crime scene, complete with yellow tape, until after the autopsy. Too many workplace crimes lately."

" I can't believe all this is happening." Cody's rosy little lips gaped open like a hungry baby bird while Chelsea spooned the strained chicken and carrots into his mouth. He started fussing when his mother moved too slowly. Her eyes softened as she paused to wipe the mess from his face. Were it not for this beautiful little being, she might be tempted to lapse into depression. She glanced at Mandy as she reached for the jar of applesauce. "I don't know how I'll manage staying in Memphis for two weeks. I've never been away from Cody that long."

"You know something, Chessie. I don't think it's Cody you're worrying about. I get the distinct impression you're more afraid of yourself than Logan Wilder. He doesn't sound like the kind of guy who would force you into anything."

Chelsea tried to look outraged, but failed. "I'm not afraid of him...physically. That's not it."

"Then what is it? You're headed for a hormone melt-down."

"Amanda Foster! You twist every thing into a sexual meaning. You're an absolute hussy!"

"Yes, and I'll proudly be one till the day I die."

"My primary goal will be to keep him from finding out about Cody. Damn, I picked up Logan in a dingy bar, went to the no-tell-motel and screwed him simple. He probably thinks I'm some sort of whore who makes it a practice to haunt the bar scene, or, or worse."

Mandy tossed her head back and roared with laughter. "That word is out of style. This is the new millennium and recreational sex is part of the dating scene. Although," Mandy added as an afterthought, "You should have had enough presence of mind to think about protection."

The inference changed Chelsea's normally tanned complexion into a blushing shade of pink. Some things were too embarrassing and private to discuss...even with her best friend. "I don't carry...you know."

"Well, I most certainly do."

"Besides, I didn't go into that bar with the intention to have sex with a stranger. I was hurt and upset. All I wanted was a couple of drinks to deaden the pain." Chelsea plucked her baby from his high chair and set him on the kitchen counter to wash his face and hands. "I don't know what I'll do if Logan finds out. He's a lawyer. Can't you figure it out? He's one of those intense, brooding types. He might file a lawsuit and say I'm an unfit mother. He could try to take my baby away from me. You see it on the nightly news all the time about fathers demanding their rights." Chelsea put Cody on the floor and he shuffled on all fours after the cat.

Mandy blew a disgusted sigh. "Hogwash on the tag of unfit mother. But you're definitely going to have to face this problem sooner or later. It's not going to vanish into thin air."

"I'll do what I have to do to prove that Daddy was murdered, and to prove that Sam and Rena did it. I'll worry about

Cody and Logan later."

"No, you better face the music now. Time isn't going to make it any easier. If you can't handle the present, how are you going to handle the future? What are you going to tell Cody when he's about eight and asks why he doesn't have a Daddy like all the other kids?"

"For someone who's admittedly a scatterbrain, you do come up with some thought-provoking points."

"How many times must I remind you that I'm not sitting on all my talent?"

"Mandy, Mandy, what would I do without your perpetual sense of humor?"

"Well, you've got until Sunday night to agonize over your decision. The longer you wait, the harder it's going to be."

***

After Mandy left and Cody was bathed and put to bed, Chelsea faced the night alone. Thoughts of her father and Redbush temporarily edged Logan from her mind. As much as she didn't want to admit it, the house where she grew up and the surrounding land were inextricably a part of her life, a part she tried for the last eighteen months to forget. The parties, all their friends, the laughter, the fun, and the happy bundle was tied together with the ribbon of her father's love. How could he have changed so much in six months? How could he choose sides with Rena and turn his back on his only child? Maybe Tom is correct in his assumption that Daddy might have been suffering from some sort of illness.

The clock on the mantle chimed eight o'clock. A shade over twenty-four hours ago her life shattered. How fleeting a condition is contentment? She'd worked so hard to keep her life together. Anyone who could juggle a drastic drop in income, a demanding teaching career, and an unexpected pregnancy, deserves some sort of award.

If anything, Chelsea was a survivor and damned if she'd let Logan Wilder sink her boat.

Chapter 5
Sunday night
Memphis, Tennessee

Chelsea spent the weekend engaged in an agonizing battle with herself. Even as she sped along the dull stretch of Interstate highway, she was still wrestling with the underlying reasoning for going to Memphis.

Was it the tantalizing lure of her father's money, the drive to find his killer, or was it to keep Logan in Memphis for the sake of protecting Cody ninety miles west in Jackson? Or perhaps it was all or possibly none of the above. Her mind was in total turmoil. What if he tried to coax her to bed? Would she be strong enough to resist? Those and a dozen other "what ifs" rattled around in her brain as she drove west into the sunset.

Oh, Mandy, why are you so disgustingly right all the time? I'm molding my life around my fear of discovery. I should have stood up to Logan, she softly agonized, *tell him in an unruffled, rational voice that our association would be strictly business with no socializing and definitely no reminders of the night we spent together. Instead, I stuttered like a star-struck teenager. Where, oh where is calm rationality?*

"Great theory, but I don't possess anything even remotely connected to calm." Her voice carried above the soft buzz of the radio. "What has this man done to me? Did something unique click between us, or was he just one of those rare men who had honed his sexual skills into an art form? Great! Now I'm reduced to talking to myself."

In the end, she made the decision to first find her father's killer and, second, to fight Rena for the Hollander estate. It would be a delicate balancing act to work with Logan, all the while trying to make certain he didn't worm his way into her private life.

Late Sunday afternoon, she'd packed the car full of Cody's "necessaries," his high chair, his car carrier, and his toys, plus a two-week supply of diapers and baby food, and moved him in with Mandy's mother. In the ten short months of his life, she'd never been separated from him longer than the hours she spent at work. Cody was such a good, happy baby, always smiling, cooing, and chattering his little nonsensical words and it was wrenching to leave, but she trusted Ellen Foster to take good care of him. Mandy promised to stop by the house daily to feed and look after Katie-the-cat.

**

She was pleased to see Tom Guthrie sitting in the lobby when she arrived at the Holiday Inn. He had called her Saturday morning with an invitation to dinner.

"Tom, good to see you. I hope you haven't been waiting long."

"Not at all. Punctuality was always one of your strong

points." He dangled the key. "I've already checked you in and the bill is taken care of for as long as you care to stay."

"Let me hang up my clothes and freshen my makeup. Give me a few minutes."

Fifteen minutes later, she emerged from the elevator with a relaxed smile. "I probably brought too many clothes, but I didn't know what you had planned."

"Court appearance and funeral for certain."

"I'll need to buy something black. Is your knee bothering you? I'll be glad to drive."

"I came with a chauffeur."

As Tom and Chelsea emerged from the hotel lobby, a silver-gray Mercedes with darkened windows pulled alongside the curbing. Tom opened the front car door. "You ride up front with Logan, I'll take the back seat."

"Lo-Logan?" She balked as a cold wave of dread washed over her in spite of the sultry summer heat. "You didn't mention that Logan was having dinner with us. I thought it was going to be just you and I."

"I knew you wouldn't object. After all, he's going to be handling this case. Logan's got some ideas he wants to discuss."

"I'll bet he does," she muttered softly.

Inside the restaurant, Chelsea pulled Guthrie aside as Logan spoke to the maitre d'. "Tom, please don't bring up the subject of Cody. My indiscretion is none of Logan's business. I don't want him to know that I have a child."

"You have nothing to be ashamed of, my dear. Single-motherhood is common place these days."

"Tom, please," she whispered with urgency. "I'm begging you."

Although Justine's was known for its fine French cuisine, Chelsea was too nervous to notice the elegantly prepared food, afraid that Tom would forget and accidentally mention Cody. Mostly the conversation was centered on Tom's recollections of happier days at Redbush. Occasionally, Logan would reach across the table and touch her hand, reminiscent of the night that refused to budge from her memory. With his tender, knowing glances and quiet smiles, it was as though he were attempting a reenactment. Chelsea slipped her hands into her lap and kept her attention glued to Tom, trying her best to ignore Logan's random intrusions into Tom's leisurely stroll down memory lane as he chatted away.

Finally, the meal dragged to a conclusion and they dropped Tom at his apartment. Being alone with Logan was something she had hoped to avoid, but her arguments to be taken directly back to her motel went unheeded by either man. Chelsea had the distinct feeling that Tom was trying his hand at matchmaking.

"My house is just around the corner," Logan stated. "I'd like to show it to you. I've done a lot of work on it and I'm rather proud of the way it's turning out."

"No thanks. I think I'd better go back to the motel. I'm very tired and need to get a good night's sleep before...before tomorrow's court appearance."

"It's early," he urged. "This won't take long."

Even though she continued to protest, he turned down Central Avenue and into the garage at the rear of his property. Logan helped her out of his car. The sun had sunk below the horizon, leaving a thin band of pale pink. His hand resting on the small of her back created a surprisingly powerful surge of emotion. Chelsea read it as a possessory gesture. The man was far too nice, too suave, and too good-looking to be ignored. In fact, everything about him was too perfect; and she had been too long without romance. During their wild night of uninhibited sex, he had generated a level of passion she had never experienced before. Her predicament? The desire to relive that night was deeply buried, but straining for release.

Damned hormones! I will not let Logan into my life. I will not let him find out about Cody, she silently repeated the pledge. Maybe if she said them often enough, she would heed her own advice. *Dammit!* Afraid that her rambling thoughts might spill into her eyes, she jerked her gaze from side to side. "I don't think-- No, this isn't going to work. Please, take me to the motel." In the darkened garage, she inched backwards toward his car, but he grasped her arm and directed her toward the back door with firm gestures.

"Nonsense. Come on. There are a few things related to the estate that we need to discuss. There's also the matter of a contract to be signed between us."

Reluctantly, Chelsea allowed herself to be escorted through the rear door. The modern kitchen contrasted sharply with the ancient exterior of the colonial-style house. Beautiful light-oak cabinets and gleaming white and chrome appliances complemented the imported tile flooring.

"Oh," she gasped, stunned to see the photos of herself affixed to the refrigerator with a magnet. "Where did you get those pictures?"

"Tom gave them to me the other day."

"That one was taken by the pool at Redbush. That's Daddy, Tom--and Emily Guthrie is in the lounge chair. She was sort of like a mother to me after mine died. The other photo was taken about four years ago when Daddy gave me the Jaguar for Christmas."

Logan watched with fascination as her expressive eyes softened when speaking of her father and of happier days.

"Have you been inside the house?" she asked.

"No, but I'd like to see it. Tom has told me so many stories about the place. As you witnessed tonight, he doesn't need much provocation to reminisce about the past. You know how old men are." Logan slipped out of his suit coat, pulled off his tie and released the top button of his dress shirt.

"Daddy was that way too. He loved telling stories about how he and Mother met, and their honeymoon in Key Largo."

"'We had it all. Just like Bogey and Bacall.'"

She smiled at Logan's off key attempt to sing, and more of her tension eased. "Something like that. They went scuba diving and found the pearls for this necklace. Daddy gave it to me when Mother died."

Her hand traveled absentmindedly to her throat as she fondled a necklace of small, irregularly shaped pearls. It was an often-repeated gesture. Logan couldn't shake the persistent image of how gorgeous Chelsea was when wearing nothing but that necklace--innocence and passion rolled into one neat little package. Chelsea was much shorter than his six-foot-two-inch frame; and her pale green summer-weight dress was clinging to her soft, flowing curves and became non-existent in his mind's eye. Her diminutive size spawned lust and a few other unnamed and unspoken cravings.

"Chelsea?" He whispered her name, softly on a small breath of air, smoothing the harshness of the first two letters, and ending with the hint of a question.

It was delightful sound, so different from his sensuous mouth than from any other source. No one in her life had ever put so much passion into her name. Chelsea didn't mean to meet his gaze, but she did. It wasn't her intent to look sexy or seductive, but she did so unknowingly. Nor did she want to reveal her vulnerability, but it radiated outward from her dark violet eyes. Her lips parted and moved, as if to say something, but she didn't. The urge to kiss him and to be kissed came hard, like a powerful fist in her gut.

It took every ounce of determination to turn away from him and switch her attention to the wood cabinets. "O-oak is my favorite wood," she stated lamely and ran her fingers over the finely grained surface.

"Usually I try to salvage the old cabinets, but they were too far gone. Come on, let me show you around. Watch out for fresh paint." He led her out of the kitchen, through the dining room and into the front hall. A ladder, tarp and several gallons of paint were parked in the sparsely furnished dining room. Pride in his accomplishments colored his voice as he pointed out the subtle features of the stately old home: crown molding, hand-carved mantle, elegant brass doorknobs and sparkling crystal chandeliers.

Along the way, Logan popped the on-switch of his stereo, flooding the lower floor with soothing music. "I've wired built-in speakers in every downstairs room and a two-way intercom throughout the house."

Do his talents have no end? she wondered.

A narrow staircase made two turns in its convoluted journey to the second floor. The upstairs hall branched off in opposite directions. The second level floor was highly polished hardwood; and their footsteps created an echo as they walked.

74

"Most of this old barn is empty. My exercise equipment occupies one room. You should hear the floor groan when I work out."

As Chelsea paused to look at a collage of baby pictures, two boys and a girl, the resemblance to her son tugged sharply at her conscience. Pointing to the one that looked the most like Cody, she asked, "Is that you?"

"Hey, good guess. My sister made these up for me. She thinks pictures give the place a homey look. These are some old school photos. If you can believe it, I was a skinny kid when I graduated from high school. Too small for football, not tall enough for basketball, so I played baseball. Then I took up weight lifting my freshman year in college."

Chelsea couldn't fathom his well-built body being anything other than strong and sensual. Sensual? Was that a Freudian slip of her thoughts? No matter how hard she fought, his predatory male grace accelerated her heart rate.

Logan continued his monologue as they proceeded down the hall. "I keep a couple of the bedrooms furnished for company. Occasionally, my nephews come for the weekend. There are only two bathrooms upstairs, one at the end of each wing. If I were going to live here permanently, I'd change that."

"If you don't mind my being nosy, why do you need such a big house if you live alone?"

"I don't. This is sort of a hobby. This is the third one I've owned. I buy them at tax auctions, do renovations in my spare time and then sell...hopefully for a nice profit. This place has been more of a challenge than I anticipated. I've been at it for nearly a year. It should be finished in about six more months, then I'll sell it, find another old house and start the whole procedure over again."

"If you're looking for a real challenge, maybe you'd like to have a go at Redbush. Rena ruined it. My recent memories of the house aren't very pleasant."

"Wood and brick are incapable of projecting a bad influence. Only the people in it."

"I don't agree. Rena painted the master bedroom walls red and put red shades on the lamps. She remodeled the bathroom with a red jacuzzi. And wait'll you see the mirrors on the ceiling above the bed."

"A little garish for my tastes. You can see that I've got plenty of room. My bedroom is at the opposite end of the hall, so you could have stayed here with your virtue intact," he stated jokingly. Her deep frown coaxed him to change the direction of the conversation. "I'm glad you made the decision to fight Rena for the estate."

He stood in the doorway of one of the bedrooms, his arms folded casually across his chest. Chelsea's gaze hesitantly met his piercing dark brown eyes. She recalled their unnerving capacity to bore directly into her hidden thoughts, which at the moment were decidedly unchaste. Her memories of their night together were playing havoc with her self-control. "It was Mandy, my best friend. She was fundamental in...well, to be honest, she badgered me into making this decision."

That was a blatant lie. Chelsea had made the solitary decision to come to Memphis to prevent Logan from following her to Jackson and possibly finding Cody. She hadn't delved deeply enough in her thinking to imagine what Logan's reaction might be to his son. He might demand visitation, joint custody, or DNA testing. Anger. Or maybe denial. At the moment, denial was her most dominant condition.

"Give my thanks to Mandy. If you hadn't come to Memphis, Tom suggested that I go to Jackson in person to find you."

See? she thought smugly. Her decision was neatly justified. There was a great deal of comfort associated with having everything in her life properly pigeon-holed.

They returned to the kitchen and Logan filled the coffee maker. He motioned her to a chair. "I've rearranged the schedule on two existing court cases so I can devote my full attention to the Hollander case this coming week."

Her eyes filled quickly with fear. "Oh, no! You don't need to do that. I thought I'd spend some time with Tom."

"No problem. We'll be in and out of the office. But we do have to be in court tomorrow morning at ten."

"I forgot to talk to Tom about that at dinner tonight," she

said. "I'm not sure I want to go through with this."

Logan frowned. "Don't you want the right to bury Claude next to your mother? Rena said she was going to cremate his body, take his ashes to Florida and toss them into the sea."

Chelsea drew in a deep breath, still finding it emotionally difficult to handle matters associated with death. "Yes, of course, but to be blunt, I don't have the ready cash for the sort of expensive funeral Daddy deserves."

"The Court will order that your father's estate pay the final burial charges. That's the law."

"I didn't know that. I've never been faced with a situation like this before. In a way, maybe Daddy did a disservice by keeping me so well isolated from life. Mandy makes fun of my upbringing. She calls it the 'Ivory Tower Syndrome.'"

"Chelsea, you've got a big stake in the outcome of this legal mess."

"The mess is probably of my own making."

Logan arched a skeptical brow. "Probably?"

Chelsea managed a muted chuckle. "Did Tom tell you about my big break-up with Daddy?"

Even though Logan knew, but he was curious to hear her side of the argument. "None of the gory details."

"It's almost funny in retrospect. I insulted Rena's cooking on Thanksgiving Day. The turkey was dry and the dressing was a soggy mess. When I voiced my opinion, Daddy demanded an immediate apology, and when I wouldn't give her one, he kicked me out of the house--permanently. Christmas passed, then New Year's. My damnable pride kicked in. I should have made the first move and apologized, but my blasted ego got in the way." Chelsea sagged into a wooden kitchen chair as the unpleasant memories flowed over her. "In February, he cut off my allowance, canceled my car and health insurance, closed all my credit card accounts, then he sent the sheriff to the grade school where I teach to repo my Jaguar. I was so embarrassed I nearly died on the spot. I guess I should be grateful he didn't try to take away my house. But I have a small trust fund from my mother's estate that Daddy couldn't touch. It comes directly from a bank in Italy. It isn't huge, but it helps keep the wolf from banging the door down."

Logan could visualize her embarrassment and it tugged at his heart--she had not only endured, but survived. It also muddied his ego. He preferred to think that his male magnetism wooed Chelsea into his bed that night, and not her private misery and anger.

"Hindsight is great, isn't it? I know I should have swallowed my pride and apologized for Daddy's sake. But Rena was sitting there looking like the cat that swallowed the canary. I was mad enough to chew nails. Instead, I drowned my troubles in vodka."

"Orange juice, vodka and sex. Very good sex as I recall."

The reminder brought a hot, swift sexual rush, and she

hoped it didn't show. "It was a childish act of rebellion. Nothing more, nothing less."

"You were anything but childish that night."

She nudged her chin a few notches higher. "I'd appreciate it if you wouldn't mention it again."

"Why? It happened, you can't deny that. Nor can you deny the pleasure we shared and enjoyed. Either that or you're a damned good actress." Logan leaned back against the kitchen counter with lazy arrogance. "You're too defensive. It was a delightful evening between consenting adults. I can't understand why you're so uptight about it."

She stumbled in her haste to rise from the kitchen chair. "Please, I've asked you politely not to mention that incident. I have my own...personal reasons."

"A man? A boyfriend, fiancé? What personal reasons?"

Determined to avoid answering his questions, she nudged her chin even higher. "If you mention it again, I'll be forced to ask Tom to switch the matter to another attorney."

"Okay. Truce." He held his hands upright in a mock gesture of surrender. Although surrender wasn't on his mind-- unless it was hers. "Come on, sit down," he cajoled. "Look, before we drop this subject completely, let me apologize for something. It's been bothering me since Friday. I shouldn't have brought up the subject of our night together in front of Tom. But...I was so shocked when I saw you sitting there that I couldn't think straight.

The details of that wonderful night just came flooding back. I know it was bad taste on my part and I'm sorry."

Chelsea sagged into the chair and stared purposefully at her hands clenched tightly in her lap. He was still standing, towering above her. She could feel those dark brown eyes of his burrowing beneath her feeble attempt to remain calm. "Yes, that did upset me. Tom is...well, he's old-fashioned. He still thinks of me as 'Claude's little girl,' rather than a grown woman. Especially a woman capable of making such a bad mistake."

"I don't think he caught the drift of our conversation. He's been so distracted by the arthritis in his knee that all he does is count the hours between his pain pills. With that said, let's stick to business. After you left Friday afternoon, Tom spoke to Larry Miller; he's the attorney representing Rena. Apparently Claude hired a new lawyer a few days after your argument. Miller has a will he alleges is newer than the one Claude signed four years ago. Rena is the sole beneficiary. We need to get an injunction to prevent her from dipping into the Hollander piggy bank while the matter is being adjudicated. At least we should lock up your father's investments and life insurance."

"On what grounds?"

"We'll allege that Claude signed the newer will under duress, and ask for a continuance until the autopsy is completed and the results of the blood and urine toxicology tests come in. I know this isn't easy for you, but we'll get through it." His tone softened. "Together. If all else fails, we can file a 'wrongful death' suit in civil court against Rena and lock up the assets for several years. By the way, Tom has tried for two days to get in touch with Walter Scruggs, but he's not answering the phone. I'm beginning to worry."

"What am I reading in your voice?" Chelsea asked.

"Hunch? Suspicion? I can't give it a name."

"Walter called me about three on Thursday afternoon. He was whispering...like he was frightened. Do you think Walter might have seen what really happened to Daddy?"

"If Walter saw them killing your father, then yes, they'd have to silence him--permanently."

"No, that's too frightening to think about." She pinched her eyes closed against the image swirling in her mind. "Walter is such a dear soul. Right now, I can't cope with the thought that he might be dead as well as Daddy. He's been looking after me since I was born."

"Well, four or five million bucks would tempt anyone to commit murder."

Chelsea blinked away the cobwebs of her private thoughts. "That much? I never knew enough about Daddy's finances to put a dollar amount to his worth."

"That's just touching the tree tops, a rough estimate that Tom came up with. It could be a lot less if Rena has been doing much spending. It's also possible that she and Sam have been squirreling money into secret accounts out of town or out of the country. Are you aware that after Claude remarried, he switched all his investment accounts to another broker? It surprised the hell out of Tom."

"Yes, he told me. But it's strange behavior. Daddy and Tom were such good friends for so many years. He was always so busy running his construction company, he relied on Tom to keep track of his portfolio, insurance policies on himself and his employees, and all the other nitpicking things. Daddy must own a dozen or more parcels of land scattered around the area. Keeping up with taxes and insurance was more than he could handle. He depended on Tom."

"After he finished that office park in Bartlett, your dad disbanded his company. Must have been about fourteen months ago. Put a lot of guys out of work."

Chelsea frowned, shocked by this new revelation. "Disbanded? Hollander Builders? That's, that's so hard to believe. You'd think Daddy's money-grubbing little wife would have pressed him to make more money for her to spend. You know, he started his construction business with three employees. It's impossible for me to comprehend what happened to Daddy to cause such a drastic change in his personality. I wonder if Jerry Bruce knows anything. He was Daddy's foreman from the beginning. They were also very close friends--boating and fishing buddies."

"We'll add Bruce's name to the list of possible witnesses. I like to overwhelm my opposition with as many credible character witnesses as possible."

"How will that help our cause?"

"People who knew Claude before and after Rena's appearance in his life can testify to the changes in his personality."

"There are others. A professional cleaning crew of three women came in every Monday to clean house and do the laundry. Daddy also had a gardener who worked five days a week. Maintaining the pool and fifty acres was a full-time job. Then there was a mechanic who worked on the vehicles and boats. There were others as well."

"Do you remember any of their names?"

"No, but they were probably paid by check."

"If Rena won't cooperate, then I'll subpoena all of Claude's financial records." Logan stepped to the kitchen counter and poured the coffee. "Cream and sugar as I recall."

Chelsea nodded then accepted the cup that Logan prepared, wrapping her hands around the heat.

"Do you remember the breakfast we had sent up to our room at three in the morning? Eggs, bacon, sausage, potatoes. We were starving." Once again Logan saw the intense anger flair in Chelsea's eyes. Another forbidden subject.

"I need to talk to Walter. It's important to find him, to make sure he's safe. I know he'll be able to answer most of our questions."

"If he's not in the caretaker's cottage on Redbush land--assuming he's still alive--"

"Oh, I can't even think about that possibility."

"Well, he could be hiding somewhere fearing for his life. Do you know anything about family members he might be visiting?"

"He was very close to his granddaughter, Doralee, but I don't know her last name or where she lives." Chelsea suddenly brightened. "Say, I've got a great idea. Let's go to Walter's house. He kept a personal journal--a combination of diary and address book. Important papers and such. He was orderly to a fault. We might find a clue as to where she lives."

"We can't. Rena was so mad about our injunction concerning Claude's body, she had her lawyer issue a restraining order against you, Tom and me. If we place one foot on the Redbush property, she's vowed to have us arrested. You were so anxious to leave, you probably didn't hear her barrage of threats and accusations."

Silent thoughts occupied Chelsea for a few moments as she sipped the coffee. Logan was right about Friday afternoon. Her mind was so jam-packed with fear and rage all she could focus on was escape--in big, bold capital letters. "The most important thing is to find Walter. Solving that will be simple, we'll search his cottage without her knowledge or consent."

"How will you do that with your evil stepmother ensconced in the family mansion?"

"Mansion? Funny, that's what Daddy called it, but I never liked that title. It conjures visions of a tall house, with dark, ghostly spirals. For most of my life, I called it home." Her voice trailed off into silence. "These days I think it's called 'a rancher.' Long, rambling and all on one floor."

Logan was getting used to her long pauses while she fought for control by staring pointedly into her cup. She needed to cry or yell, he thought, or whatever it takes to release her grief and anger. "How do you propose we get on the property unseen?"

"A midnight raid. You can't see the cottage from the main house. Besides, I know every acre, every trail like the back of my hand."

"That's illegal."

"You're the attorney. Can't you figure out a way to get around the law?"

"I've spent my career upholding the law, not breaking it."

"Never mind, I'll go alone."

"No, I won't allow that."

"You can't tell me what to do."

Logan's shrug was a helpless gesture. She was right. He could only advise her; and she was obviously too headstrong to accept his advice.

"Before we go any further," she stated, her voice

defensive. "I want to get a few things settled between us. Let's keep this strictly on a business basis, nothing personal."

"That's the next item on tonight's agenda. I have a standard contract between lawyer and client that you need to sign." Logan put his briefcase on the table and withdrew a printed form. "I'll represent you to contest the will. If something doesn't show up on the tox report, it won't be easy to prove that Claude Hollander signed it under coercion and duress, but we're going to give it a try. We'll cross file with the older will. If the autopsy suggests murder and we're lucky enough to get a conviction against Rena and Sam, then my job would be a lot easier. Read the contract at your leisure and if you agree, sign it. If you have any questions about my handling of the estate, air your gripes and we'll discuss them with Tom. This isn't written in stone. Any time you're unhappy with me, you're free to find another attorney or even another law firm if you want."

After a cursory glance, Chelsea signed the paper, rose from the chair and carried her empty coffee cup to the sink. Staring through the window into the dark night offered a temporary calming effect. Cody.

I'm here because of him. There's so much I want to give my son. Security. Advantages. Everything I had. Cars, clothes, and all those other little niceties that only money can buy. Entry into the best college, fraternity, spring breaks in Vale or Acapulco. I want him to concentrate on his studies and not have to work.

Logan's voice jolted her out of her thoughts.

"This is a moral issue, even more than monetary," Logan stated. "By all appearances, Rena's a little tramp. I briefly met your father a few years ago when he came by the office to see Tom. It takes a giant leap to imagine what an educated man like him would see in Rena Wheeler."

"Sex," she snapped.

Logan laughed aloud with pure devilment sparkling in his eyes. "Yeah, sex is great, but...it's nice to have someone to talk to when you get out of bed."

"Rena was so different in the beginning, when Daddy first started dating her. Her hair and clothes were different. Her voice was softer then, and she used better grammar, that's for certain. After what I heard Friday, I can only assume it was all a big charade."

"Claude Hollander wouldn't be the first older man to be taken in by the sweet voice and soft touch of a much younger woman."

"The first time I met her, I didn't actually dislike her, I only thought she was way too young for Daddy."

"Pure and simply, she probably instigated the relationship for money. Chelsea, you should be the rightful heir, not her. You and...your descendants."

In Chelsea's slanted perception, he said the word "descendants" as if he knew she had one. Once again folding her hands in a prim manner, Chelsea kept her eyes averted, wondering if "motherhood" was visible to the naked eye.

"I'd like to show you something." Logan left the kitchen and returned with a huge aerial photo encompassing the entire Redbush estate. "Tom told me that after you left to teach school in Jackson and before he married Rena, Claude toyed with the idea of selling off a portion of his land, so he had this aerial photo taken."

"Oh, my goodness, look at that. I've never seen it from this viewpoint." When Logan laid the large glossy black and white photo on the table, Chelsea leaned over it and traced the familiar landmarks with her fingertips, her eyes softening. "There's Walnut Grove Road, White Station Road. It was owned by the Hohenbergs before Daddy bought it. All fifty acres...it was as if the rest of the world didn't exist outside these walls. My bedroom had a view of the pool. There's an herb garden right outside the kitchen door. See this barn? When I was little, I had a beautiful palomino mare. I called her 'Bunny.' Original, huh?" She spoke in a whispery voice, as though lost in reverie. "I was so sad when she died, I cried for days. Even though it was against the law, Daddy let me bury her beneath the corral. Walter's cottage is tucked away in the trees over here," she pointed. "You can't see it from the main house. Oh, this brings back so many memories. It seems so long ago."

Logan paid more attention to her eyes than her words. There was that rare spark. He yearned to keep that light burning with even greater intensity and overpower her pain. He fervently wished he could protect her from the more gruesome aspects of this case--wave a magic wand and poof, the matters concerning her father's death and his estate could be resolved without further heartbreak for this beautiful and fragile young woman.

"What's this?" she asked, pointing to a cluster of buildings.

"A new apartment project. It butts along the southern edge of the property line."

"I don't remember that."

"I recall Tom telling me about a zoning battle."

Chelsea sat down, she was quiet for a long time, engrossed in her thoughts, then finally asked, "In your own mind, do you think Daddy was murdered?"

"The autopsy will be performed tomorrow. That's the first critical test."

"I know, I know. It's not murder unless the coroner says it's murder." Chelsea glanced at her watch. "It's getting late, I need to get back to the motel. It's been a long day and I'm tired."

The stereo system that Logan had turned on when they arrived went silent, clicked forward to the next compact disk, then filled the house with the rich, full-bodied tones of a concert piano. She was quietly reflective for several minutes, transfixed by the sheer beauty and simplicity of the solitary instrument as it enwrapped her with sound. She was fully immersed in the fluidity of the music as she visualized the lean hands and long, agile fingers executing the complicated melody.

"Mom tried to pound culture into our heads when we were kids," Logan said quietly, as if embarrassed.

"Van Cliburn," she whispered. "He never attacks the keyboard, he--"

"--caresses it," Logan finished her sentence.

Chelsea locked with his gaze. The impact of the intimacy of the word "caress" was as powerful as the knowledge of the sensitivity required for a person to read that attribute in the musician.

Logan unfolded his tall lanky body, stepped around the table, grasped her arms and lifted her into a standing position-- maybe too quickly, maybe too roughly, but she didn't withdraw. As he lowered his head, she tipped her chin to look up at him. Their gazes locked again. The veiled passion in her eyes, her womanly scent, her warm proximity, all joined forces to nudge their way beneath the surface of his composure. The sexual rush caught Logan off guard. His blood was drumming in his ears. The gap between their lips narrowed. To kiss her, to taste her--those were his only thoughts. Not of their delightful past, nor of what he hoped might be in their future, but only the here and now.

He held her face between his hands as tightly as the music held captive her soul. He gently captured her mouth with his, savoring again what he had been wanting to savor since she had come back into his life last Friday. Her lips parted to greet his probing tongue. She tasted so good. Coffee, sugar, and passion. One hand dug into her silken hair, the other slipped around her shoulders and took her prisoner, determined to never let her free. No other woman he had ever known--young or old, shy or bold--had the power to engender such a turbulent kaleidoscope of feelings. His grip on her shoulders lessened and his hand slipped down her spine to her bottom, pressing her into full contact with his body. He lifted his mouth slightly, his eyes and voice smoldering with desire.

"Nothing has changed. It's the same as before," he whispered, then pulled her into another formidable kiss.

Although both of Chelsea's hands were trapped between their bodies, they seemed to have a mind of their own, sliding over his hard chest, his broad shoulders and around his neck. The fast, chaotic thump of her heart mixed with the rising and falling crescendos of Rachmaninoff's music and drowned all thoughts of resistance. The crystal-clear tones of the piano mingled with the desire that flowed hotly through her veins. To hell with the consequences, to hell with tomorrow. She would be content to stay here forever, but knew that it had to stop and stop now.

When she finally pulled away, she spoke in the professional tone often used with her young students, although a trifle more shaky and breathless. "You shouldn't have done that. You keep breaking the rules, Logan. This is one rule that should be written in stone. I don't understand what you want from me. If your agenda has anything to do with a probable future relationship, then we better have a parting of the ways right here, right now."

Logan paused before responding, struggling to compose himself. "My professional agenda is to protect your legal rights against Rena Wheeler Hollander. I can't deny that personally I see you as a beautiful woman. I can't forget the night we shared, nor stop my imagination from dreaming of a possible future. No arguments, no threats or promises can force me to forget or deny my dream. That's something you need to understand, Miss Hollander." Logan's grip on her shoulders tightened.

In the bright kitchen light, she could plainly see the intention in his dark eyes. Yes, common sense told her she should drop the subject and retreat but she was too angry to back down. "There are two sides to every story. You probably went to the bar to pick up a woman. I went there because I was angry, hurt that Daddy would take sides with Rena against me."

"In my own defense, I went to the bar that Thanksgiving Day because I was lonely. My parents and sister had gone to Europe on vacation; my brother and his family were out of town as well. Until I saw you, I had no intention of picking up a woman, but you looked as lonely as I felt. Understood?" When she nodded mutely, he released her. "Come on, I'll take you back to the hotel." Logan picked up his car keys and reached for her arm. "Whoa, wait a minute," he exclaimed. "You must have leaned against a wall and smeared wet paint on your arm. Let me clean it off."

He guided her into the downstairs bathroom with the light pressure of his hand in the middle of her back and invited her to sit on the toilet lid. The bathroom was in total disarray. Large sections of wallpaper had been steamed from the walls and an assortment of tools was scattered on the crumbly linoleum floor.

"Excuse the mess, I've been painting for two days. I only have my weekends to devote to the house." He sat on the edge of a claw-footed bathtub and gently dabbed at the paint spots with a damp cloth. "Chelsea, I sense that you're afraid of me," he stated. "But I can't figure out why. Yes, I guess I've been guilty of taking advantage of our situation, but please understand that I mean you no physical or mental harm--far from it."

The soothing softness in his voice matched his gentle touch and created a deceptive calm. "No, I'm not frightened of you." That was only a partial lie. She was frightened of his power to generate a sexual response. "It's just that this is an odd situation for me. I've never been inside a man's house. I mean, that is...." Chelsea clamped her mouth shut, fearing she had inadvertently revealed too much.

"You've never been engaged or had a live-in lover? How could a young woman as beautiful as you avoid romantic entanglements? Guys must have been lined up outside your door."

"I don't know about that, but, but I don't think my past relationships are relevant," she stated defensively. In this day of the liberated career woman, she was embarrassed to admit that she'd never had a serious relationship. "Before the split with my father, I had always thought that the guys I dated were only after Hollander money or a job with Hollander Builders. I guess I don't have to worry about that anymore."

Logan stood up. "Let's go."

***

Several hours later, Chelsea lay between the cool sheets on the motel bed still awake. She was tired, but not sleepy. There was too much traffic noise, the air conditioning, people walking in the hallway. When added together, it was too distracting. The room was cloaked in blackness, no street light, no moon, no reassuring night light. If that weren't enough, her racing mind added to the melee, concocting a new assortment of "what ifs."

She continued to toss and turn. She missed Cody so much it was driving her mad. Tomorrow evening she would call him. He was at that age where the telephone fascinated him. He would listen to the voice coming through the instrument with wide-eyed wonderment. Thinking of his bubbly laughter brought a smile to her lips, but the smile quickly faded as she stared into the darkness.

Whether or not she wanted to admit it, she and Logan had spent a night together and created a child. She couldn't forget the experience. Every time she looked at him, the memories loomed larger than life. Every newly revealed facet of his personality only added to his overall appeal as a lover, husband and father. He was a good man. She knew that beyond doubt. He didn't deserve the lies. Although Rena was the one and only catalyst for her toboggan ride into hell, by Chelsea's own doing, she was weaving a web of lies that was threatening to come unraveled. Her flimsy house-of-cards was about to come tumbling down around her.

Damn Mandy for being so disgustingly right again. When Cody grows old enough to ask questions about his father, what would she tell him? Could she risk his disgust and say she didn't know his name? Or say that he died? But if he pressed his search, he would learn she had lied.

Sleep was very late in coming.

Chapter 6
Monday morning
Memphis, Tennessee

Chelsea, although somewhat pale, looked every inch the daughter of a wealthy busnessman when she and Logan stepped inside the courtroom. She was wearing a royal blue tailored suit, and her matching high heels made her appear taller as she walked down the isle beside Logan, who was equally well attired.

Rena Hollander and Larry Miller, her young, inexperienced attorney, were already seated at the long table reserved for counsel and their clients. Miller was no match for Logan Wilder's poise and powers of persuasion.

Since there were the unresolved suspicions of foul play, the judge ruled in Chelsea's favor and ordered Claude Hollander's body be released to his daughter following the autopsy. Furthermore, he forbade cremation.

Rena's shrill opposition rose above the banging gavel, and before the lawyer could silence his distraught client, she was ruled in contempt of court and fined. If looks could kill, both Logan and Chelsea would have been struck dead on the spot by Rena's venomous glare. Although judges were ordained by law to be impartial, this one had apparently taken an instant dislike to Rena's overt brashness.

Rena filed the most recent document naming her as the

sole beneficiary of the Hollander estate and Logan counter-filed Claude's four-year-old will written prior to his marriage to Rena. The judge also signed the injunction to freeze all of Claude's assets until the case concerning the contested will could be prepared and scheduled for trial.

Rena jumped up a second time. "I gotta have money to live on," she shrieked.

The judge lost his patience, ordered a small monthly allowance and levied a second fine for her conduct.

***

Logan guided Chelsea out of the courthouse, past the press of media, and into the quiet safety of his car.

"What do all these reporters want?" she asked.

"The public loves a juicy story. Old man, young wife, angry, disinherited daughter, money, maybe even murder. News is more entertainment these days than the telling of facts. It's a game of ratings for the networks. You may think I invited you to stay at my place because I had seduction on my mind." He reached across the console and squeezed her hand. "I won't lie and say the thought hasn't crossed my mind...repeatedly, but I am concerned about your comfort and safety."

"Safety? Surely I'm safe in a hotel."

"Big money is paid for a story with pictures. They'll probably follow you everywhere for the next couple of weeks, ask

98

questions, and shove cameras in your face. They'll search the personal history of everyone associated with this case, digging for dirt, always looking for something sensational."

Bubbles of fear danced wildly in her stomach. Her beleaguered thoughts were freshly assaulted as her vivid imagination ran amuck. "But, but, I have a right to my privacy."

"Not in their eyes. Look what happened to Princess Diana. If it weren't for the media, she might still be alive today. One of the first big cases I handled for Tom when I was right out of law school was the 'Snuff Heiress' divorce. She was a fading opera star and her ex owned the company that processes tobacco leaves into snuff. What a circus! My face was plastered all over the TV nightly news and the morning papers. Tom was horrified at first until he realized it was great free advertising. People were flocking to our doors with their legal problems. We'll just have to wait and see how this scenario unfolds. To help protect your identity, Tom registered you under his name."

She leaned back in the seat and closed her eyes, hoping to block out reality, and not caring what their destination might be.

Thirty minutes later they stopped by to confer with Tom. The suite of offices was in a state of bedlam, forcing Chelsea and Logan to side-step paint buckets, ladders and electricians.

"Your father's signature looks a little shaky," Tom noted as he compared the old will to the new one. "Check out the differences."

Chelsea studied the firm, bold handwriting on the will he'd written four years earlier, with the wobbly-formed letters on the current one. "Was Daddy ill? Do you think he was on some sort of medication?"

"The toxicology report will tell us that," Tom explained. "Brew tells me the tox report sometimes take as long as three weeks. I do know for a fact that certain cardiac medications don't mix well with antihistamines. The drug interaction can cause mental confusion. There are probably hundreds of other lethal mixtures lurking on the drugstore shelves."

"According to the police report a bag of pill bottles was collected from the residence," Logan explained.

"Daddy was never the sort to take pills--not even vitamins."

"We might try to locate Claude's family doctor. Do you know who he is?" Tom asked.

***

"No. His old doctor died and I have no idea who he was seeing. I remember that Daddy was involved in a minor construction accident and had to go to the Emergency Room to get his hand stitched."

"When?" Logan asked.

"Before he married Rena, and before he kicked me out of the house. Maybe his medical record has some clues. In fact, that's

100

when he met her. The way I understand it, Sam was working for Daddy and drove him to the Emergency Room. Rena must have been working there. Apparently, she went by the house that night and made a big to do about redressing his wound. I guess all that tender attention went to his head. I had already moved to Jackson, so I don't know exactly how everything developed."

"Is Rena a registered nurse?" Logan asked with amazement glittering in his dark eyes. He pulled pad and pencil from his suit coat and scratched a few notes.

"I'm not sure, but I don't think so. How much education does it take to change a bandage?" Chelsea shook her head from side to side. "Nothing about Rena adds up. She put on such a convincing act of being a sweet, soft-spoken lady. Maybe...maybe if I'd stayed in Memphis none of this would have happened."

Logan placed a reassuring hand on Chelsea's shoulder, his fingers tightening slightly. He knew she was wrestling with her guilt, blaming all the failed "I-should-haves" on herself.

Tom leaned back in his chair, lost in thought. "Wonder if he could have been suffering from the first stages of Alzheimer's? Doctors have pills to treat that disease now--or at least slow it down somewhat. Claude went through such a drastic personality change the last eighteen months of his life. He terminated all his relationships with old friends--not just me. He also folded his company, hired a new lawyer, new stockbroker, new accountant. I'd give a pretty penny to know what was going on inside Redbush during these last two years." Tom sighed with resignation. "I guess we'll never know the truth."

The unsettling thought that her father might have been ill, and that she wasn't there to comfort him, was worrisome and added more weight to Chelsea's already heavy load of guilt.

"Damn, we really need to talk to Walter Scruggs." The old leather chair squeaked when Tom heaved himself from the cushions. He moved around his large desk and approached Chelsea. He lifted one chilled hand from her lap and clasped it between his own warm hands. "Claude's body will be released sometime tomorrow. You've got some decisions to make. Casket, flowers, someone to do the eulogy, pallbearers, church. I assume you'll want to bury him next to your mother."

"I, I--" Chelsea drew in a deep breath trying to stave off the flow of tears.

"Would you like me to handle everything?" Tom asked.

She was flooded with relief and, at the same time, added a few additional pounds of guilt. "Can you?"

"Of course, I had to do it for Emily, I can do it for Claude. You two run on. I'll take care of everything. Oh, by the way, Susan said she saw a media van parked at the Holiday Inn on her way to work this morning. So be careful. They might start following you."

"I thought I spotted a tail when we left the courthouse," Logan stated.

The nightmare seemed to be getting worse by measured

increments. "Have you tracked down Walter yet?" Chelsea asked as she rose to leave.

Tom shook his head slowly. "No, I was hoping he'd contact me, but not a peep."

Chelsea appeared dazed as Logan guided her across the parking lot and into his car. She sagged into the supple leather seat of the Mercedes, glad to let others bear the weight she was apparently unable, or unwilling, to handle for herself. During the last two years, she had handled herself competently when she was disinherited and faced an unexpected pregnancy, but there was always the tantalizing thought in the back of her mind, that she and her father would ultimately have reconciliation. But now, because of Rena, that happy day would never come to pass.

She rolled her head to stare at Logan's profile. The strong set of his jaw made her feel so physically safe, and yet so emotionally battered. First and foremost she wanted to see that Sam and Rena paid dearly for what they did to her father. Then, and only then, would she deal with the subject of Logan and Cody. By the sins of omission, she had already lied herself into a corner. Once again she fought the seemingly ever-present threat of tears.

Even with his attention on driving, he could sense her looking at him. "There's a place I'd like to show you," he said. "It's a bit of a drive into the suburbs, so close your eyes and relax."

***

The crunch of a gravel driveway awakened Chelsea from a light nap. Her eyes blinked open and she scanned the surroundings to get her bearings. "Where are we? The place looks deserted."

"It is. It's where I grew up. Been in the Wilder family for generations. My mom and dad sold it last year. I wanted to buy it, but I had just bought the place I'm in now and didn't have enough cash. My dad retired at the end of the year and is planning a move to Florida."

"Who owns it now?"

"A corporation called Mid South Development. I guess they acquired it for future development. A subdivision, apartments, shopping center, who knows."

"Oh, Logan. That old farmhouse...it's beautiful. It would be a shame to bulldoze it."

"The main structure was built in 1887, but it's been remodeled, updated and added on to several times. Come on, maybe we can get in through one of the back windows."

They both slipped off their suit jackets as they emerged from the car. Logan loosened his tie and released the top button on his shirt. Chelsea kicked off her high heels. And, after making certain that Logan was looking the other way, she even shimmied out of her panty hose in deference to the hot humidity of Memphis in June.

The weeds were thigh-high as they circled to the rear of

the house. Vandals had broken through the kitchen door that was hanging open. Hypodermic needles and litter from drinking parties were strewn on the dusty oak floors. High ceilings and crown molding gave the interior an elegant ambiance.

"I'm itching to get my hands on this place. I'd knock out the wall between the kitchen and dining room. What do you think?"

"Oh yes!" Chelsea was drawn into his excitement. "Build one of those floating islands."

"Install a bay window for the breakfast area."

"With a view of a flower garden and some kitchen herbs."

"I'd build an attached garage over there." He pointed. "Enlarge the master bedroom, the closets and bathroom."

"Oh yes, with one of those fancy garden tubs."

"There are four more bedrooms upstairs," Logan explained as he ushered her toward the narrow stairwell.

"It's got so much charm and potential. Which was your room?" She was totally mesmerized as he told amusing stories about growing up with a brother and sister. Chelsea visualized the interior as she could make it look. Something about the place touched her heart. She'd traveled the world and had never experienced such an intense sense of belonging to old brick and wood. She experienced coolness where there was no breeze, and warmth where the sun didn't shine. Not even Redbush with its Hollander family history had such a calming aura.

"These bedrooms could be for the children--two girls and two boys. Tom keeps telling me to get busy and start a family before I get too old." When Chelsea whirled around to face him with near terror clouding her eyes, he halted abruptly. Concerned, he asked, "What's wrong? What did I say?"

Fear curled around her heart. "N-nothing. A-a spider. I'm barefooted and I thought I saw a big spider."

As she tried to hurry away, he slipped his arm around her waist to restrain her. "Come on, I'll show you around the property." They retraced their steps to the outside. "The original tract was two thousand acres, but over the years, it was sold piece by piece. Now it's only forty-five. My grandparents raised beef cattle and gaited horses." A boyish excitement shaded his voice as they left the house and walked along a weed-choked path.

The eastern horizon was a dark, purplish blue; the western sky was blood red and the canopy above was a riot of puffy clouds painted in weird shades of reflected light. They leaned against the top fence rail of the corral, enjoying nature's display of spectacular colors and the scent of grass and wildflowers. His hand tightened around her shoulders, tucking her snugly into the crook of his arm. For the moment, nothing else mattered to him except these few quiet moments of sharing.

The gesture was simple, his arm around her, but Chelsea read it as another in a string of subtle acts of ownership. And damn her soul, she liked it, that feeling of belonging to someone, of

106

being half of a pair. She wished he were greedy and disagreeable, with a huge assemblage of annoying habits. But no, Logan was a good and honorable person, and she knew beyond all doubt that he would be a loving and caring father to their son. But that would have to be a distant image, because to realize that dream, she would have to traverse a path of fiery coals...with bare feet. Pulling away and desperate to break the spell, she said, "It's a shame you can't buy it back from the developers."

"Corporations are damned determined to make a profit. When I sell my house, I'll have enough to swing it. You might go so far as to say this is my Redbush. The place where my memories are." He swung her around to face him, gently resting his cupped hands over her silk-clad shoulders. "I've got this theory about memories. You can pack the bad ones in a trunk and put them away in the attic, but every time you move, you have to drag them along. So, you might as well learn to live with old memories: the good, the bad and the ugly."

He looked down at her with a fresh supply of unspoken intimacy shining in his eyes. He couldn't get this close without the ache to kiss her, to make that physical connection between their bodies. He lifted his hands to cradle her face. He brushed his lips across hers, half expecting her to protest, but was happy when she didn't. "I've been thinking about you, about us for the last eighteen months. I started missing you when I woke up and found you had gone without a trace. I didn't even know your name or where you lived, but you left me with one hell of a memory."

She lifted her head and stared into his deep-set brown eyes, darted with flecks of gold. They seemed to possess the unnerving capacity to burrow deeply into her soul and read her private thoughts. She wished mightily that she could read his. Was it pity? Concern? Or something else?

Can he see my weakness?

With slow hesitation, Logan combed his fingers through her hair and cupped the back of her head with his broad hand. She had the freedom to break away, but didn't. Her pink tongue flicked out to moisten her lips, as if in anticipation of the kiss he longed for. He bent low, tipped his head to one side and pulled her mouth into delicate contact with his lips. The kiss resumed without complaint--tenderly, softly, but with hungry intensity. Passion was restrained at first, but then he let it flower and blossom. Control cracked and slipped away, replaced by urgency. He wanted more than a taste, more than a sample as he molded his body to hers.

A quivering sigh fluttered almost noiselessly in her throat as flames raced through her body. His touch created a tidal wave of need and she was hard pressed to deny the damp heat. She kissed him back, with all the love and desperation in her heart. Through the haze of passion, she managed to refocus on reality and pushed against his chest. "Logan, please. I asked you not to do this."

"What's wrong, Chelsea? What are you afraid of? Why do you respond, then push me away?"

She twisted free, ran to his car and huddled as far away from Logan as the physical restraints of the vehicle would allow. He drove her to the Holiday Inn in unsettling silence.

***

In the motel parking lot, Logan spotted two men were leaning against the WHBQ-TV van, drinking coffee and engaging in deep conversation, so he pulled around to the rear entrance.

He killed the engine and twisted in the seat to face her. "Will you talk to me rationally for a few minutes?" he asked.

"About what?"

"About us."

"No."

"No?"

"Shall I spell it? Logan, the only ones at issue right now are Sam and Rena. Not us. Not now."

"I'll pick you up at ten in the morning," he stated matter-of-factly.

Chapter 7

Tuesday

Logan arrived at the Holiday Inn promptly at ten the next morning and they went to the restaurant on the main floor.

"Did you sleep well last night?"

"Yes, thank you. After you left I called Tom and had dinner with him."

Logan felt a hot twinge of jealousy, but kept quiet about it.

"We discussed Daddy's funeral arrangements...among other things. It's odd that I can talk to Tom with more freedom than I ever had with Daddy."

"As kids, we always worry about parental censure."

"What are we going to do today?" she asked as they read the breakfast menu.

"The autopsy results are in."

Chelsea's eyes sparked with a mix of curiosity and fear. "And?"

"Brew, my dad, is going to meet us at the Forensic Center. We'll both find out then."

"I've been wondering why you use his given name."

Logan smiled. "I deal with him quite often on a professional level, and I didn't think it was cool to call him 'Pops,' or 'Dad.' You might feel more comfortable calling him Detective or

Lieutenant. Whatever suits your fancy." Chelsea returned his smile, although to him it appeared somewhat wistful. "What did you call your dad?" he asked.

"He was always Daddy to me, except the last time...then I called him a stubborn, senile old fool."

"That bothers you, doesn't it?"

She neither responded nor met his gaze. "I think I'll have scrambled eggs and toast. I'm hungry this morning."

Later, on their way to the lab, Logan knew they were being tailed. "Damn, they nailed us today."

"Who?"

"The local TV station. Now they know what kind of car I drive. We'll just have to put up with them. Hopefully, this will all be over in a couple of weeks. Maybe sooner."

* * *

The Shelby County Forensic lab was housed in a large, modern building in the northern suburbs, a good distance away from the Main Police Precinct at Jefferson and Third. Although she grew up in Memphis, this was her first trip inside this facility. It didn't look much different from those in the cop shows she'd seen on TV. Everyone was wearing white lab coats and clacking away at computers. Apparently, no one used old-fashioned typewriters any more.

That Brewster Wilder had been a handsome man in his

111

youth was still evident. There was no doubt that the two men were closely related. In spite of his age, he retained a touch of boyishness in his face. Although his hair was stark white, it was thick and slightly unruly. Chelsea could plainly see where Cody inherited his good looks. Once again she was gripped with the possible unfairness of her decision to keep Cody isolated from the Wilder family. He had no grandparents to dote on him. Would he be less loved because of that void? Would he feel the same loneliness that she felt from growing up without an extended family? She felt a twinge of sadness, regretting the absence of aunts, uncles and cousins in her own life.

Brewster shook her hand. "I'm sorry we have to meet under these circumstances, young lady," he stated. "Murder investigations, especially those concerning immediate family, are never pleasant."

"Then you do think he was murdered?"

"Yes, it looks that way."

Chelsea's hands clinched into tight fists. "How?"

"Drowning, and there was head trauma as well, but I'll let the Medical Examiner explain the details."

"It's Rena and Sam," she muttered. "I knew it, I just knew it."

"Do you know anything about this Samuel Wheeler who is also living on the Redbush premises?"

"He was introduced as Rena's brother, but they don't look

112

anything alike. He moved in about three months after she married my father."

"Does he work?" Brew asked. "Or does he mooch?"

"He did have a job with Hollander Construction, but that was a couple of years ago."

"Hmm, wonder where all the old company records are," Brewster mused. "I'd like to get his social security number."

"Tom Guthrie had the corporate records up until...say...two years ago, that's when I moved away. I don't know where they are now. You know, I thought Sam Wheeler might be into selling stolen cars. There were always two or three fairly new vehicles parked in the garage. Every time I came to visit Daddy, it seemed he was driving something different, and none of them had license plates."

"I've run the name Samuel Wheeler through the main computer and couldn't come up with a firm match in Tennessee. I did find one guy with the same name and a rap sheet down in Jackson, Mississippi. I'll order pictures and fingerprints. In the meantime, we'll keep digging. Come on, let's go to the Medical Examiner's office. He can explain everything to you better than I."

The autopsy room lay in gruesome brilliance beyond a pair of double doors. She was relieved when Lieutenant Wilder led them away from it and down a long corridor flanked on both sides by dozens of cubicles with white-coated workers leaning over high-tech equipment. But when she got a full whiff of formaldehyde and all the other noxious odors, her stomach did a flip.

"These are the technicians performing tests on trace evidence," he explained.

Brew made the introductions. "This is Doctor Leo Zambini, the medical examiner, and this is my son, Logan Wilder, and his client, Miss Chelsea Hollander, the victim's daughter."

Zambini stood, smiled and shook hands. "Have a seat. I think I have some very good news for you. According to the statement from the victim's wife, she claimed her husband went to the pool for his daily early morning swim. She theorized that he must have slipped on the pavement, hit his head on the concrete edge, and fell in and drowned. Yes, he did drown, but he was hit and hit hard before he got to the pool."

"Where, how?" Chelsea set her squeamishness aside as she listened intently to the man's explanation.

"When I palpated the injury on the side of the victim's head, I found a depression fracture that seemed to have a triangular shape. At the center of the depression, I observed a break in the skin, about eight-and-a-half centimeters. I also found flakes of blue-colored metallic material in the wound."

"Wait a minute," Logan interrupted. "I have a report made out by the first officer on the scene that mentions a blue vacuum-packed brick of coffee."

"That's right." Zambini shuffled through his papers.

114

"When that first officer was talking to the widow, she offered him a cup of instant coffee, joking about her lack of cooking skills. The officer was trying to keep the scene secure until the coroner and Homicide Detectives arrived and he noticed the unopened brick of coffee on the counter. He thought it odd that she had fixed him the powdered stuff when she had real coffee."

"Do you think a brick of coffee was the murder weapon?" Chelsea asked. "Is it hard enough?"

"Yes, if it's vacuum-packed."

"Rena is small. Daddy was large and well built. Only Sam would have the strength and power to hit Daddy hard enough to crack his skull and kill him. But, if the coffee brick was the murder weapon, why would they leave it in plain sight?"

"Why not? It would draw less attention. The criminalists are going to do a Luminal test at the residence tonight in search of blood-splatter evidence. We'll get a search warrant so we can bring in the brick of coffee for testing. And, if we have a match with your father's blood, hair and skin, then it looks like we'll have enough evidence to issue an arrest warrant."

"How exactly did my father die?" Chelsea asked, her voice unsteady.

"Death was due to drowning after a cerebrovascular accident."

Chelsea lifted her hand as if she were a student. "May I have that in plain English, please?"

"The blow to the head caused a rupture of the cerebral vessel which in turn caused a stroke--closed head bleeding. It's called a Berry aneurysm. There were no plaques in his carotid arteries. There was no evidence of Alzheimer's disease in his brain-stem tissue where there's usually some signs of deterioration. Nor were there any other obvious disease processes going on in his body. In fact, for all intents and purposes, Claude Hollander was a healthy man. What did not fit the scenario of natural causes was the depression fracture and tearing of the skin. I would judge that he lost consciousness immediately, then apparently he was put into the swimming pool where he drowned." Zambini paused and his expression softened for an instant. "I can assure you that he was not conscious and that he did not suffer."

"That's comforting." Chelsea managed to bestow a pocket-sized smile.

"I might add that the injury does not match what we would expect from hitting his head on the concrete edge of the pool."

"The pool at Redbush is made of smooth ceramic tile--not rough concrete. What about the confusion and change in personality?" Chelsea prodded, barely hanging on to her composure.

"The blood and urine toxicology report will tell us if there were any drugs in his system that might have contributed to an altered mental state. That takes anywhere from two to four weeks.

We have a collection of pill bottles taken from the residence. Some were samples of prescription drugs, some over-the-counter products. Muscle relaxants, antidepressants and blood pressure medicine, especially MOA inhibitors, are notorious for serious drug interactions. Even if we find toxic combinations in the screening, it's still hard to prove in court who administered the medicines and their intent to do harm. I know how difficult this is for you, but please be patient. Those tests take awhile to complete. I'll advise Lieutenant Wilder as soon as I get the results."

"Thank you, Doctor. I appreciate you taking the time to explain everything to me." Chelsea, Logan and Brew walked back to the second floor hall near the elevators. "When can Sam and Rena be arrested?"

"Not right away," Brew stated. "First we need to do the Luminal procedure and run tests on that brick of coffee."

"Can't you charge them with something?" Chelsea asked.

"Right now we don't have enough hard evidence to prosecute. The two suspects don't know the results of the autopsy yet. We're going to bring them in for further questioning tomorrow morning. They claim they were sleeping when the incident took place, and yet Wheeler made the call to 911. We'll try to break apart their alibi one piece at a time. Hopefully under questioning, one of them will slip up. The head wound Hollander sustained would produce a small amount of blood splatter," Brew continued with his explanation. "A team is going out to the crime scene tonight. Even if Rena washed the walls and pavement, the blood droplets will show up under the testing chemicals with a special light."

"What about Walter Scruggs?" Chelsea asked.

Brew opened the file and shuffled through the papers. "Scruggs. Oh yes, he's the old man who found the body. He lives in the caretaker's cottage, right? I've got his statement. What else is going on?"

"He called me at work--in Jackson--last Thursday afternoon to tell me about Daddy...dying. His voice was whispery and secretive, like he was afraid someone would hear him. He asked me to come see him as soon as I got to Memphis. I tried, but the main gate was chained and padlocked. We've been dialing his number since last Friday, but he hasn't answered his phone. Rena got an injunction against Logan, Tom Guthrie and me. Can you get on the property and search Walt's cottage?"

"Not without 'probable cause,' especially if Missus Hollander is being uncooperative."

"Isn't the fact that a murder was committed 'probable cause?'"

"Not necessarily. The law was meant to protect the innocent and isn't always fair in dealing with the guilty."

"Apparently, there's no justice in the justice system," Chelsea snapped.

"If you can get his next-of-kin to report him missing, then

we'd have 'probable cause' to search the cottage. Missus Hollander will have to let us on the property to conduct tests. Otherwise, it will appear she's hiding something. Miss Hollander, while you're here, maybe you'd like to see your father, have a few minutes alone with him," Brew suggested. "Now that forensics has finished their investigation, the body can be turned over to a mortician for embalming."

When the color drained from Chelsea's features, Brew Wilder regretted his offer. He was too used to dealing with death on a daily basis and it had made him somewhat callused. "I'm sorry." He lightly touched her shoulder. "You don't have to do it now. But it's an important part of the grieving process to see him. You need that closure."

Talk of morticians and embalming pushed Chelsea over the limit of control. She launched herself into Logan's arms. Without thinking of the consequences, she locked her arms around his neck, buried her face in the collar of his suit coat and allowed the tears to fall. The sterility of their surroundings faded out of mind and sight.

"It's okay," Logan whispered into her silky hair. "It's okay." It pinched Logan's male ego to think that her reaction would have been no different had he been Tom Guthrie or Walter Scruggs. But a new emotion claimed his consciousness, that of being needed. His hand, with fingers widely spaced, skimmed across her back, then tightened and drew her closer.

Brewster Wilder sensed he was an accidental witness to the beginning of something...love perhaps, he thought whimsically. About time his youngest son found a ladylove. He walked away, whistling softly, without a speck of his earlier regret.

***

Bright flashing lights blinded Chelsea as she and Logan emerged through the double glass doors of the forensic facility. Microphones were shoved into her face and a barrage of questions assaulted her ears. Logan bulldozed through the crowd and hurriedly pushed her into his car.

"I never knew that detective work could be so exhausting," she groaned as she kicked off her shoes. "I thought dealing with preteens was stressful."

"What shall we do for dinner?" Logan asked as he pulled away from the parking lot.

"I'm more tired than hungry. Would you take me back to the motel? I want to change clothes and get my car. I'm going out to Redbush tonight. I don't care what you say."

"Let's go to my place first. We'll talk about this later."

"There's nothing to talk about. I don't want to hear any more of your arguments about what's legal and what's not. I don't care about that. I've got this gut feeling that Walter's life is in danger. You heard Tom. He agrees with me on this point. He told me last night how worried he was. I want to get to him before Sam and Rena do. Yes, I know it's dangerous, but Walter is a dear soul and needs our protection. We've got to do something before it's too late. If you won't help me, then I'll find him on my own. You can say no all you want, but it's falling on deaf ears."

"You win! Okay? You win. We'll leave about midnight. Damn, you must have been a terror as a teenager." Logan blew out an elongated breath of air as he pulled into the motel parking lot. "Damn, would you look at that?" There was someone dozing in a car parked next to Chelsea's Chevy. "There's one on our tail and one waiting on us."

"How do you know that's a reporter?"

"Who else would be sleeping in a car in this kind of weather?"

The meager shade from a row of spindly loblolly pines was too scant to offer much relief from the heat, she observed. "Yes, but how does he know it's my car?"

"Department of Motor Vehicles, better known as the DMV. The reporters probably know your life history by now-- schools you attended, how much you owe on your credit cards. It's downright scary how much information is available these days."

And the name of Cody's pediatrician, she anguished silently. Fear had taken up permanent residence. "Go around back. I'll run upstairs and change into jeans and sneakers. I'll meet you back at your place. To heck with them." Chelsea's hand began to tremble as she reached for the door. She could feel the fabric of

121

lies beginning to unravel.

Thirty minutes later the Mercedes and Chevy pulled into Logan's garage behind his house. In the daylight, she could see that Logan's penchant for neatness extended into his garage. Ladders, tools and such were all hanging neatly in place. From the look of the contents of the shelves, he also changed his own oil and did other minor vehicle maintenance. His talents were seemingly endless. Did the man have no flaws at all? A new tidbit of information to pass on to Mandy...check out the neatness of a man's garage before committing to a long-term relationship.

In the living room, Chelsea sagged into the deep cushions of the sofa, too tired to move. She scooted lower, kicked off her sneakers and propped her feet on the heavily scarred coffee table.

"Why don't you grab thirty minutes of shut eye?" Logan suggested. "I've got some paper work to do and a few phone calls to make."

Chelsea nodded, but her mind was too active to allow her the luxury of a nap, or even to relax for a few precious moments. Too many things to fret over. How long would it take those reporters to follow the trail back to her house in Jackson and eventually to her son? How many days or hours until Logan would see the story on the front page of the Memphis Commercial Appeal or on the nightly TV news? She could envision the "Scandal Rags" at the local supermarket having fuzzy pictures of Cody taken with a telephoto lens. Although she had no intention of sleeping, fatigue

122

caught up with her and after rearranging her position, she curled up on the sofa and drifted into a restless nap.

Later, when Logan finished working, he went into the sharply shadowed living room. The house was dark. Weak rays from the kitchen light angling through the doorway created frightening forms from the innocence of furniture. Chelsea's loveliness filled his entire heart. It hit him with startling force--he was falling in love. In fact, if the truth could be admitted, he had been in love with her since that fateful Thanksgiving Day encounter. Until the very last days of his life, he wanted to see that face every sunrise and every sunset. The memory they created that night would ride the last beat of his heart. The feral, primitive need to nurture and protect was so potent he felt thoroughly helpless. Her full lips were slightly parted--wet, warm and inviting. This was no illusion as he watched her heavy breasts rising and falling each time she inhaled.

As he knelt down to watch her sleep, her eyes--a ridiculous mix of purple purity and violet passion--fluttered open and she focused her gaze on him. Flames ignited as he cradled her face in his hands. There was less than six inches between their lips as he whispered her name. "Chelsea, Chelsea, why won't you let it happen?" He didn't want to stop until he made love to her, until he was buried deep inside her. He maneuvered their positions until they were laying body-to-body, full length on the sofa.

Chelsea was fully awake as she felt his hand slide beneath

123

her tee shirt and release her bra. Her nipples puckered in response to his touch. He moved his hand between her legs, the harsh denim fabric was a rude barrier. She arched at his touch, leaning into his hand, groaning softly with her need, and locking her arms around his neck. Her lips parted with an invitation to his tongue. It was the same as before. His lips, his touch could make her forget everything but her desire, her need. The sharp memory of their exquisite joining made her want to experience it again, and again. With her free hand she untucked his shirt and groped for his bare flesh. His muscular body was hot beneath her hands.

The sound of the zipper on her jeans jolted her from the haze of need into reality. She scrambled from the sofa like a frightened fawn and straightened her clothes. "This isn't going to work, Logan. You keep breaking the rules." Her voice cracked and trembled as she spoke.

"To hell with rules. I can't get near you without wanting to make love to you."

"I think you better learn some self-control."

"Why do you respond to me? Why do you return my kisses?"

His eyes turned hard, then soft again, as the blatant fear in her eyes made him hang his head low in remorse. The house was wrapped in its silence, only Logan's sharp intake and exhale of air could be heard. The atmosphere was thick, heavy with raw emotion.

"Look," he finally whispered. "Go upstairs to one of the spare bedrooms and rest. I won't bother you again. That's a promise I'll keep."

***

In the solitude of an upstairs bedroom, Chelsea gathered her wits and decided to call Ellen Foster to see how Cody was getting along. She wanted to hear his bubbly laughter. It always lifted her spirits and at the moment, her spirits were in desperate need of elevation. She carefully dialed the long string of numbers from her credit card so her call would not show up on Logan's phone bill.

"Yes, Mrs. Foster, this is Chelsea. I'm registered at the Holiday Inn under the name of Thomas Guthrie. Room nine eleven. I'm trying to dodge the media. They were taking pictures and everything." She paused to listen. "They what? The evening news in Jackson? Oh Lord! Whatever you do, don't take Cody anywhere near my house. Look, I'll be tied up for at least a week--I don't know for certain. Do you need any additional money to cover costs? Keep a record and I'll reimburse you. Is Cody awake? Wonderful. Will you put him on the phone?"

She waited until she heard his giggle and said "Mama."

"How's my big fella? Are you staying out of trouble?" He responded with a few unintelligible gurgles. "Yes, Cody, sweetheart, I love you very much. Goodbye, honey, I'll talk to you

125

in a couple of days."

The moment Chelsea hung up the phone, she knew she was being watched. Her head swiveled around to see Logan standing in the doorway.

Chapter 8
Tuesday night

"You might as well come in," she told him, frantically wondering how much he had overheard.

He stepped across the threshold. "I apologize, I didn't mean to eavesdrop on your private conversation. I heard your voice, the door was hanging open, and, and--"

"Forget it." She tried to slough it off. "I don't have any secrets." Lying never set well with her conscience, but she rationalized that protecting Cody was more important than the truth.

"Chelsea, I didn't know you had a serious relationship going on with someone back home. Why didn't you tell me at the outset?"

"I don't have anyone," she blurted recklessly, then immediately regretted her impulsiveness. For once, another lie would have served her better.

"Then who's Cody?"

Her mind flip-flopped through a string of possible responses.

My dog, my cat, my godchild.

"Cody is...he's someone I know back home. Nothing serious."

"'I love you very much' sounds serious to me." She

attempted to brush past but he grabbed her arm and twirled her around to face him. "A few minutes ago you certainly weren't acting like you were in love with another man. Dammit, why won't you be honest with me? Every time I turn around it seems as though you're fabricating another story."

She studied the highly polished hardwood flooring while silently agreeing that her lies were piling up like a cord of firewood. One slip and it would all come tumbling down, burying her alive. His hands, so warm through the fabric of her tee shirt, moved to her shoulders. The feelings were too comforting. All she had to do was lean forward a few inches and she would be in contact with his strength, his body, but she held herself rigid and unmoving.

He possessed the power to make her forget all the bitterness trapped inside her heart since the breakup with her father and the unrelenting grief over his death. Only her full confession and Logan's absolution could smooth the raw edge of guilt over the ever-growing web of lies. But the painful reality of her situation was that if she embarked on any kind of relationship with Logan, he would eventually see his son. Then she'd have some tall explaining to do. It was slowly evolving into a no-win situation. Even if she told him the entire truth right this instant, she would still be the loser. So no matter which path she decided to take, she doubted that he would ever find it in his heart to forgive her deceitful behavior.

Her lungs began to burn and she realized she'd stopped breathing. She closed her eyes and sucked in a breath of fresh air. "I have an active life back in Jackson," she stated flatly. "And a great many friends--men and women."

"Is that roommate you mentioned the other day a man?"

"I don't have to explain myself to you. Okay?"

"Okay, okay." Logan released her, but his frustrations were bursting at the seams. "Look, I'm not much of a cook," he explained. "But I can fix bacon and eggs if you don't want to go out to eat."

"Food. Yes, that would be good. Can't remember if we ate lunch," she said and followed him downstairs to the kitchen, grateful for the change of topics.

"Tell me more about Scruggs' granddaughter," Logan urged as he prepared to scramble a skillet full of eggs.

"She's a little older than I, but the same size. I used to give her some of my clothes."

"How old are you?"

"My birthday was last month, I'm twenty-eight now." Chelsea banged around in the cabinets and drawers until she found plates and silverware. "Doralee was wild as a teenager--got pregnant a couple of times. She lived with Walter occasionally. I hated the way she trashed her life. Walter said she got mixed up with the wrong crowd and couldn't seem to say no to drugs. She was so sweet tempered and pretty back then, but heaven knows what time has done to her. Even when she was drinking, Doralee always came to see her grandfather every Sunday night. It was a ritual engraved in stone. Both her parents are dead. Walter's love was the only stable thing in her life. He'd dry her out, give her a good meal and a few dollars and she went on her way."

"Maybe she knows where Walter is. Maybe he's hiding with her."

"I hope so. He sounded so urgent when he called last Thursday. The whispering tone of his voice really haunts me. Say, that call would have been long distance. Can you subpoena Walter's phone records?"

"When there's sufficient probable cause."

"Such as his disappearance?"

"Yes, that would do it." After consulting his notes, Logan tapped in Walter's phone number and let it ring ten times. "He's still not answering. If he's not there in the middle of the night, then where is he?"

"Doralee moved around so much, there's no telling where she is now. I don't even know her last name. I'm sure it will be listed in Walter's personal journal."

After they ate and straightened the kitchen, Logan checked the time. "It's almost midnight. The police should be finished with their Luminal test. Are you ready to go to Redbush?"

When Chelsea looked at him with excitement streaming from her eyes, he realized that he wanted to be the man who kept that glow where it belonged and replaced the shadows of sorrow.

"Really? No more arguments?"

"Would it do any good?" Logan asked.

"No! Do you have a flashlight and compass?"

"Yes, and I'll bring bolt cutters. There are two strands of barbed wire atop the brick wall."

"That must be a new addition."

"Our biggest problem will be leaving my house unnoticed. Have you looked out the front window? That damned reporter has been glued to our butts."

"What are we going to do?"

"I've got an old pickup truck I use for hauling lumber. It's parked behind the garage. This neighborhood was built when garbage was collected from a back alley. The alley is still there, overgrown, but passable."

***

There was no place to park on Walnut Grove Road. The houses were old but stately, with lush Bermuda lawns ringed with azalea bushes. Logan's old truck, parked in this wealthy neighborhood, would draw suspicion, something they didn't need; so they parked in the new apartment complex. Carrying heavy gloves, a compass and armed with a flashlight and a pair of bolt cutters, they walked north toward the southeastern edge of the Redbush property.

"I hope no one calls the cops on us. We could never

explain ourselves. In fact, I could get disbarred."

"Believe me, an arrest warrant wouldn't look good on my resumé either. Teaching is my livelihood." Chelsea was glad for the darkness as she remembered breaking the news to the principal that she was pregnant and unmarried. She was lucky not to have been fired. Fortunately, Cody was born two weeks prematurely. Although rushed, she was able to recover her figure and be on the job when school started four weeks later in September. She couldn't afford the luxury of breast-feeding since Cody had to go immediately into day care.

As if clairvoyant, Logan stated, "Any teacher fired on a morals charge could file a lawsuit."

"Are you ambulance chasing, Mister Wilder?"

"Sometimes I get carried away with my profession. I like to represent the underdog fighting the system. Nothing gets my blood stirring like a get-down-and-get-dirty fight."

"Like me against Rena?"

"Correct." The eight-foot brick wall circled fifty acres of Hollander land. It was a private oasis of dense trees smack in the middle of suburbia. The wall and wire were imposing, but not unscalable. "Is it electric?" Chelsea asked.

"I don't see any resisters or insulators, only the barbs. Keep your fingers crossed that it's not connected to a silent alarm system," he said as he slipped on heavy work gloves.

Logan vaulted to the top, cut the wire, then reached down,

132

grasped Chelsea's arm and hauled her up. She hooked one hand around his neck as she struggled to regain her balance on their lofty perch. Even this incidental brush of flesh, generated a formidable response, seemingly affecting every cell in her body.

"Stay where you are," he ordered. "Let me go first." After he was safely on the ground, he said, "You jump and I'll catch."

She held on to the rough-edged brick with her curled fingers as she dangled over the side. Logan tightly gripped her hips and eased her to the ground. The thick stand of trees on the perimeter had never been pruned or cultivated. Honeysuckle and thorny blackberry bushes had grown wild and unchecked beneath the tall pine and oak.

"Walter and I used to come to this corner of the property every Fourth of July and pick wild blackberries. He'd bake a cobbler--tart and juicy. I can almost smell it."

"You do have a few pleasant memories of your childhood."

"Other than when my mother died, I had a great childhood. Truthfully, my bad memories didn't begin until Daddy married Rena. Then life went to hell in a hand basket."

"Are you sure you know your way around in the dark?"

"All I need is a quick look at the compass. If we head due north to the wall, then west, we'll come out at Walter's back door. The main compound is closer to the southwestern boundary of the property."

Chelsea held the flashlight while Logan used the bolt cutters to prune a rudimentary path. She followed close behind him pointing the way as they battled through the tangled underbrush. Outside the small but calming circle of light, dark shapes without detail snagged their clothing. She seemed so comfortable, so much at home in this miniature forest, as if that tiny portion of her remote Cherokee blood had forged to the forefront as they traversed the black copse of trees.

The crackling of twigs and leaves beneath their feet was overpowered by the raucous whine of cicadas. The hoot of an owl was followed by the muffled whir of wings as the outraged bird strafed their heads as punishment for coming too close to her nestlings. They finally arrived at the edge of a clearing and peered across the yard to the small cottage. Scattered straggly clouds offered an occasional moment of blackness. They waited for a cloud to obscure the moon light, then dashed across the open area, fighting their way through tall weeds.

"I wonder what happened to Daddy's gardener? The grounds look so shabby and unkempt," Chelsea whispered. "I'll bet the inside of the house is a mess as well."

Logan thought he would have to break into the back door, but surprisingly it was unlocked. The house was hot and stuffy. A lace-trimmed hankie muted the flashlight's glare as they investigated the kitchen. The floor was littered with broken dishes, the contents of drawers, flour and sugar from overturned canisters.

The bread had molded in the high heat and humidity of June. The inch of coffee in the glass carafe was also growing a thick crop of mold.

"What happened? It looks like a tornado swept through here." Chelsea opened the refrigerator and checked the expiration date on the carton of milk. "It was good till yesterday. Somebody was looking for something...but what?" Logan commented. "Let's search the rest of the house."

The cottage contained six rooms. Two bedrooms, bath, living room, kitchen, and dining area. Both bedrooms had been ransacked. The contents of Walter's dresser drawers had been tossed around. The clothes hanging in his tiny closet had been searched and thrown to the floor. A piece of dust-covered luggage was tucked beneath the bed.

"I can't imagine that he'd go spend time with his granddaughter and not take any clothes. Oh Lord, look," Chelsea groaned. "Here's Walter's wallet lying on the dresser."

"Looks like he left in a big hurry."

"Without his wallet?" She led the way into the living room and peeked out the window. "Walter's car is gone. At least that's one good sign."

"Where would he have kept important names and phone numbers?"

"In his roll top desk. Oh Logan, look. Everything is scattered. I'll bet it was Rena and Sam. They must have been looking for clues to his whereabouts." Chelsea sank to the carpeted floor and began searching the scattered debris. "Here it is."

"Does Rena know about the granddaughter, Doralee?" Logan asked.

"I doubt it. Walter always made her stay away from the big house."

Logan shone the flashlight over her shoulder as she scanned Walt's address book. "There she is--Doralee Jacobs, 1432 Austin Peay Highway, Maplewood Apartments, unit six. Walter kept scratching over the old addresses and adding new ones. She must have moved five or six times. The Austin Peay Highway is on the Northeast side of town."

"Oh damn, no phone number is listed. I'll call information when we get back to the house." Chelsea ripped the page from its binding and stuffed it into the pocket of her jeans.

"This could be a crime scene. We really shouldn't be scattering this stuff any more than it already is. We could be destroying trace evidence."

"Crime scene? Don't tell me you think Walter was killed here?"

"Well, I don't see any blood stains, but--"

The glare of headlights suddenly swept into view. Logan grabbed Chelsea by the waist and pulled her roughly to the floor. There were four windows in the living room--two on the side and two in the front. At the sound of slamming car doors, Logan and

136

Chelsea scrambled into the bedroom. The swinging beam of a flashlight going from one window to the next, dogged their heels, as they dove under the bed. The light, penetrating the darkness through a window, was accompanied by an exchange of male voices.

"Is this where Wheeler lives?"

"Can't be, I don't see no cars."

In the cramped area, their bodies were pressed together tightly, their limbs entwined. Logan could feel the tingle of arousal, but had no inclination to halt its progress. When she twisted her hips to find a more comfortable position, he could feel her pelvis in full contact with his erection. One hand was trapped beneath his body. The fingers of his other hand were wound in her hair and he pulled her head against the curve of his neck. Her lips were a major distraction--so close to his ear, he could feel and hear her breath coming in hot, rapid little gasps. Passion ruled as his hand moved down her back to cup the curve of her bottom pulling her even closer.

"Look around back," a male voice yelled.

Logan tensed. If the intruders went around to the rear of the house, they would discover the unlocked door.

"Naw, this place is a junk heap. Wheeler ain't here. Told me he was livin' in a big mansion. We must a took a wrong turn. Let's go back to the turn-off."

As the sound of the retreating vehicle diminished, Chelsea

tried to wiggle free, but Logan's grip tightened. "We have to follow them," she urged.

"No, we should wait."

"We have to go after them. I want to see what they're up to."

Logan reluctantly complied; and they left the way they came in.

Having grown up on this land, Chelsea knew every short cut, every path. With Logan on her heels, she hurried through the darkness around the east end of the compound, past the horse barn and tennis courts.

The sprawling flagstone house burst into full view, awash in brilliant security lights. Two wings ambled outward at ninety-degree angles on each side of the main living area. The Redbush mansion was early nineteen-fifties vintage.

Logan continued to follow Chelsea, skirting the south wall, around the swimming pool, and where the pool house apartment butted against a four-car garage. There was a covered walkway between the garage and the back door.

Logan and Chelsea crawled beneath a canvas-shrouded cabin cruiser and watched and listened as the two men they had seen earlier stepped from their car and knocked on the back door. They hunkered behind the sun-rotted tires of the trailer and listened to the exchange of dialogue. Sam Wheeler stepped outside to greet his visitors with Rena following.

"I got four vehicles for you to look at: a Cadillac, Rolls Royce, Ford Escort an' a Jeep Grand Cherokee. They're in the garage," Wheeler explained proudly with his thumbs hooked in the waistband of his jeans. "The two old ones got high mileage, but the Jeep's only got twelve thousand miles on it. Should be worth a pretty penny down in Central America."

"I don't know what they'll fence for, but don't get too greedy, Wheeler. We'll take the Jeep now and come back for the Escort later."

"Naw, take the Ford now. It's the hottest. I wanna get it off the property an' out a town in a hurry."

"What about that boat?"

"Every thing goes," Sam responded. "But not right now. There's also silver, jewelry, an' fancy painted pictures too."

Logan felt the heat of fear when one of the visitors came close to the cruiser and lifted the canvas covering the stern.

"Inboard. Old, but quality. Might keep it for myself." The man peeled several bills from a roll of money. "Okay, here's a down payment. Nice doing business with you, Sammy, my boy. We'll be in touch."

***

Back inside the kitchen, Rena shivered as she took two beers from the refrigerator and tossed one to Sam. "Whoee, I'm glad to get rid a that Ford. Do you think the cops found anything

139

with that test they done? You got any idea what they was lookin' for?"

"Just leave the worryin' to me."

"I got a right to worry. The cops made us leave the house while they was messin' around inside." Rena sniffed the air. "Smells funny in here."

"Listen, birdbrain--"

"Quit callin' me names. I'm sick an' tired a you always puttin' me down. Don't forget, I'm Missus Hollander an' without me, you don't get a penny. For two years I've had to watch ev'ry word I've said, watch which fork I picked up. Wear all them prissy clothes. I'm the one who had to sleep with the old bastard." Rena shuttered from the unpleasant memories. "Two years of him takin' them little blue pills an' gruntin' over me."

"What do you care? Isn't it better than moppin' floors at the hospital or hustlin' tricks for a pimp?"

"Not much better." Rena paced a small circle around the kitchen alternating between swallows of beer and drawing deeply on a cigarette, carelessly flicking her ashes on the vinyl floor. "Damn, I hate this place, it gives me the creeps."

"After you get the old man's money, we can fix it up. A few million bucks will do a lot of fixing."

"I don't want to fix it up an' I don't want to live here no longer than we got to. It's almost like it's full a ghosts--the old man an' his wife. Hangin' 'round watchin' us." Rena shivered again and wrapped her arms across her breasts. "I wanna sell everything--house, land an' furniture. I don't want nothin' to remind me of this joint."

"You're not calling the shots. I am."

"You try to act like you got all the brains, but I say you ain't covered our asses."

Sam's hand snaked out and laid a stinging handprint on Rena's cheek. "Shut up, bitch! I've had enough of your back talk."

Rena's tongue tasted blood in the corner of her mouth. She straightened up and stared back at him with defiance. "You're gonna live to regret beatin' up on me," she whispered almost inaudibly. "You know you shoulda killed Walter."

"Yeah, well, I woulda if I coulda got to him."

"If he saw anything, an' if he runs off to the cops, we're sunk."

"Naw, I think he was too scared. Don't worry, I'll find him. In the end, I'll find him."

Entrepreneur. Sam Wheeler couldn't spell or pronounce the word, but knew its definition fit him perfectly. He was a man who could take the tiniest window of opportunity and turn it into easy money. Of all his nefarious endeavors, it was his job at Hollander Construction that was turning into a gold mine. This was his most complicated plot, but the multimillion-dollar payoff would make it worth the trouble. Rena was a royal pain in the ass, but he would put up with her whining--at least for a little while longer. At least until he got his hands on more of the money. He squelched the desire to smile. Rena didn't know about his secret stash.

"I don't want to go down to the police station tomorrow an' answer no more questions."

"You gotta. We've been over your story at least a hundred times. You ought to know it by now."

"I want to pack up an' get the hell out of town," Rena argued. "The cops also took all them pills I was givin' the old man."

"None a them was poison. Look, for that much money, we gotta hang tough just a little while longer. We're too close to the payoff."

"All them lawyers is givin' us is enough money to run the house. We can't touch none a the big bucks until all this court shit is settled. Who knows how long that'll be."

"Look, if the cops turn up the heat, then we'll skedaddle for Mexico."

Chapter 9
Tuesday night

When Chelsea's shoulders wrenched with smothered sobs, Logan pulled her into his arms. They could see and hear the footsteps crunching the gravel as a man circled the huge cruiser, paused, then returned to the group. They waited until the money changed hands, the visitors left, and Sam and Rena returned to the house. Silence settled comfortably into the night. The outdoor lights had been forgotten and left burning, bathing the entire perimeter of the house in white-bright halogen. He released her slowly, hoping she wouldn't get hysterical.

"Calm down, take a deep breath," he whispered. "What upset you so much?"

"Th-the Ford...it belongs to Walter. Oh no, they must have done something to him."

"Shush, don't jump to conclusions. We don't know anything for certain." Logan rolled from beneath the trailer and dragged Chelsea with him. They hovered in the shadow of the old boat while brushing the leaves and pea gravel from their clothing.

"I can't help but jump to conclusions. Where is he? Where's Walter? Where would he go without his car or his wallet?"

He grasped her shoulders and shook her lightly. "Hush! They'll hear us. We'll find him. Maybe he sensed the danger and ran away on foot, leaving everything behind."

"Why didn't he call the police? Why didn't he call Tom or me? They've done something to him. I just know it."

"Maybe the phone line was cut, maybe he felt cornered. People do crazy things when they're frightened."

"I knew that Sam-bastard was into stolen cars," she hissed. "I don't understand why Daddy couldn't see what was going on right under his nose."

"When you love somebody, you don't always see their faults."

Chelsea closed her eyes and forced herself to breathe evenly in a mighty effort to regain a semblance of calm. Take one step at a time. That's what she had to concentrate on. Find Walter. Find evidence to prove Sam and Rena are guilty of murder. Then she could make an attempt to straighten out her life.

"Come on, let's get out of here," Logan urged.

"No, I want to look inside the pool house apartment. With Daddy gone, I guess Sam moved inside the big house. Eighteen months ago, he was living out here. Maybe he left some papers, names, and phone numbers. It would help to know the names of those thugs."

"Yes, it would, but dammit, it's bright as day with those flood lights shining on the water."

"I know another way of getting in. Follow me."

One of the four garage doors was left open when the visitors took the Ford Escort. Hunched low, Logan and Chelsea darted inside. Another door was located in front of the Rolls Royce leading into the kitchen of the pool house apartment.

"Daddy kept a key over the door sill. Maybe it's still there."

Logan retrieved the dust-covered key and unlocked the door. They entered the small, but luxurious living quarters. A quick search of the closets and dresser drawers in the three rooms revealed only a few toilet articles and some discarded clothing. No papers, not even a pencil. The air conditioning was running, there was a six-pack of beer in the refrigerator, but the kitchen cabinets were empty.

Chelsea plopped down on the brightly colored sofa and scanned the room looking for even the tiniest of clues. The lights from the pool, shining through the sheer filigree lace curtains covering the sliding glass door, shimmered with the subtle movement of the blue water.

Logan sat beside her, put his arm around her shoulders and squeezed lightly. Watching as she buried her face in her hands, he sensed she was once again fighting for control. "There's nothing more we can do. We need to head home," Logan spoke in a hoarse whisper.

He turned to look at her. The lacy light cast alluring shadows on her face. Something snapped inside Logan's mind. His hands roughly clasped her head. He kissed her hard and hungry. Passion exploded and he felt her quick answer to his raw desire.

All pretense of resistance melted away. This unique brand of excitement was something she had encountered only once and only with Logan. Eighteen long months ago. It had been her night of private infamy when Cody was conceived. She clung to Logan, weaving her fingers in his hair. Driven by her misery, she wanted to climb inside the man and seek the calming safety his arms had once before offered her. Her volatile needs swept away all inhibitions. She wanted him here and now. Like an addiction, she wanted to recapture the luxurious experience and the slow escalation of tension until the hurtling ecstasy saturated every fiber of her being.

The wall of propriety broke, releasing the emotions she had fought so futilely to contain. For a few brief moments, she allowed herself to forget her grief, her guilt, and her loneliness. Forget the danger of discovery. Nothing existed now except her own shuddering demands. The stiffness of her muscles relaxed and she melted into his embrace, molding her curves to his until their bodies became a single unit. The flow of chemistry was so good, so right. Her lips parted and she accepted the sweet, tentative probing of his tongue. She was drowning in the wetness of her wanting. Heat and the exhilarating sense of danger vaporized sanity and logic.

Logan's mouth traveled across her cheek, to her ear and mumbled repeatedly, "My precious one."

His lips laid a fiery trail down her neck, while one hand

slid up her thigh, grasped her bottom and pulled her against his straining erection. The other hand slipped behind her back and released the hooks of her bra. The weight of his body forced her downward onto the soft, deep cushions of the sofa. He cupped her taut breast then leaned down and lightly teased her nipple between his teeth until it hardened. The ache and burn of his physical need forced a wrenching groan from his mouth. The fierce desire to bury himself in her satin wetness, prodded him beyond endurance. He'd never felt such strong desire for a woman and was no longer in control.

His mouth on her breast launched a ripple of cascading thrills onto every sensuous pathway in her body. Chelsea yanked his shirt from his jeans, popping buttons from the fabric in her haste. She tilted her pelvis in greeting. Her hands explored his body--his broad shoulders, the deep contours of his muscles, her fingers trailed down the groove of his spine to his tight, well-rounded buttocks.

He braced his weight with one hand while the other reached down. The raspy sound of his released zipper was drowned by their heavy breathing and blood rushing through their ears. She dipped beneath his under shorts and wrapped her hand around his thick erection. Every nerve ending was throbbing with the torment to have him buried deep into the core of her body. She savored every shameful thrill.

The sultry heat of June felt almost cool against their

flame-hot skin, now covered by a slick patina of sweat as they circled in the vortex of a storm of primitive passion. She lifted her hips and started to wiggle out of her jeans. Nothing mattered to either of them now except putting out the fire.

The jarring sound of a slamming door pierced the silence. "You dumb asshole! You left all the lights on."

"Who gives a shit? We're not payin' the electric bill."

"Close the garage door while you're out there. We don't want nobody stealin' our cars." Rena's dry laugh sounded like the cackle of a chicken.

Logan and Chelsea held their collective breaths as they listened to the whine of the electric garage doors closing, followed by the remote sound of the kitchen door slamming shut. They were enveloped by sudden and total darkness. Logan collapsed on top of her, then rolled to one side against the back of the sofa. They remained where they were, with their bodies in full contact, gasping for air. Her tee shirt was rolled up and her naked breasts were pressed against the coarse hair of his chest. One of Chelsea's legs curved around his hips. His right arm was penned beneath his body, the other was resting on her upper thigh.

The loud interruption flung them back to rude reality. "God knows, Chelsea, I'm sorry. I want you, but I didn't mean for anything to happen here, like this."

Chelsea scrambled free. Unseen tears were streaming down her cheeks. She rezipped her jeans, hooked her bra and jabbed at her shirttail with jerky movements.

"They closed the garage door. How do we get out of here?" Logan asked, still out of breath.

It took a few seconds to regain her composure. "The, the bedroom window." Chelsea wiped the tears from her eyes while Logan wrestled with the latch, held tight by too many coats of paint. She climbed over the sill and while Logan closed the opening to cover their trail, she broke into a run.

He followed, the tail of his buttonless shirt flying in the breeze. He was winded by the time he caught up, grabbed her shoulder and wheeled her around. "Wait a minute!"

She jerked free and raced ahead of him. Prickly blackberry thorns tore mercilessly at her bare arms. The imposing wall temporarily halted escape. She leaned her cheek against the rough brick, gasping, nearly hyperventilating, while she waited for Logan to help her over.

**

They rode across town in absolute silence. Chelsea was so stone faced that Logan decided to keep his thoughts to himself, at least for the moment. He pulled behind the garage at the rear of the property and switched off the engine of his old pickup.

"I'm going back to my room at the motel."

As Chelsea fumbled for the door handle, he reached across her body to restrain her and wrapped his fingers around her

149

wrist like a warm bracelet. "Wait a minute. Let's talk. Maybe you're expecting me to say 'I'm sorry,' but that would be hypocritical. I wanted to make love to you since I walked into Guthrie's office and saw you there. Big as life. A dream come true."

"I'm not the same woman you met in the bar eighteen months ago. I was angry that night. I wanted to get even with Daddy. Unfortunately, I picked the wrong way to do it. Lord knows, my mistakes are legendary. I make rash judgments, sometimes I drink too much, laugh too loud; and sometimes I curse, use vile language, lose my temper and fly into a rage."

"And sometimes you respond with the passion of a fiercely hot-blooded woman. You can't deny that. Chelsea, I'm not the least bit sorry about anything that has happened between us eighteen months ago or tonight. I do regret the inappropriate location and that you're upset."

"I'm not upset. Who says I'm upset?"

"I do."

She sagged deeper into the crumbly vinyl seat of the ancient truck, tipped her head back and stared up at the display of stars against the backdrop of a black velvet sky. That's how she closed the doors in her mind, look away, count the stars or cracks in the ceiling. Anything to avoid facing the truth. Her heart was pounding so furiously she could barely breathe. The darkness, though comforting, offered little relief against the high humidity.

"I tried to make it perfectly clear that this is strictly a business arrangement. A lawyer/client relationship. Nothing more, nothing less. But every time I turn around you're breaking the rules."

"There are no rules between us. You know I'm not the type of man who would force you into anything you didn't want. What almost happened between us--several times, I might add--was one hundred percent mutual. Inside that pool house, if we hadn't been interrupted, we would have made love right then and there. We were this close." He gestured with two fingers. "You can't deny it was something we both wanted."

She knew he was right, but refused to admit it, at least out loud. In fact, everything he was saying was true, but she wasn't ready to face it as yet. "Let's forget what happened," she softly urged.

"Forget, hell. Dammit Chelsea, give us a chance. You're cutting me off from all sides and I don't understand why."

His husky tone was too distracting. "This is business: to catch my father's murderers and settle his estate. Don't try to read anything else into it. I just sort of...lost my head for a few minutes."

With a firm grasp, Logan pulled her chin around to face him. The shadows were deep across her face. "Look me in the eye."

She pinched her eyes closed, refusing to meet his gaze.

"Let go. You're frightening me."

"I don't think you're afraid of me. I get the honest impression that you're afraid of yourself."

Her eyes popped open wide. "Afraid of myself?" She turned his statement into a question. Although she tried to portray anger, at this particular moment, she was too exhausted to muster that much emotion. "How can you say such a thing? You don't know anything about me."

"I know more than you think."

"No, you don't," she whispered, taking in gulps of air. She had lied herself into a corner with no face-saving way out. "I'm not afraid of myself. I'm, I'm afraid of the truth." Her voice cracked with emotion, shocked she could verbalize such a revelation to him. Yes, the truth was screaming to be heard. The truth that she had given birth to his son. The truth that going through the ordeal alone had been so painfully lonely. The truth that she trembled from his touch and felt abandoned without it. The truth that she wanted him to love her for herself and not because she was the mother of his son.

Chelsea sucked in another quick breath and held it. *Oh no, that's it. That's the real, selfish truth. First and foremost, to be loved for myself.*

"No, my sweet lady. The truth will set you free. It's time to get beneath your anger and find out what's really bugging you. There's so much that needs to be said, needs to be brought into the open. There's a voice inside screaming to be heard."

He gently lifted her chin. Her bottom lip was quivering and he lightly sucked on it sending another wave of arousal surging to her fingertips and toes. He had the power to generate so many delicious feelings. She couldn't make herself break away. The joining of their lips was so exquisite. No matter how hard she tried to reject it, she longed for the joining of their bodies. She wanted to consume him and to be consumed.

After several minutes, a cloud passed in front of the moon, plunging them into absolute darkness. Logan's left hand moved from her chin, down her neck and encircled her breast. She clenched her fists and pinched her eyes closed again. Even through two layers of clothing, his touch was liquid fire.

He kissed her, then pulled an inch away and murmured her name, "Chelsea, I want to make love to you, with you...now, tonight. Come to bed with me, sweet lady. Let me love you the way we did that night in November. Let's make us a new memory."

She gritted her teeth so tightly, her jaw ached. If only she could listen to her heart, to the constant urgings of her body, but the trek between the car and bed was too broad, the spontaneity would be lost. It would be so damned easy to give in, to lie down right now on the front seat of this old truck and pull him into her arms. Instead, she moved his hand away from her breast. "Maybe you think I'm a tramp, someone who picks up strange men in bars and takes them to bed for sex. You probably won't believe me, but it was my first and only time."

"I knew it then and I know it now. I also know that what happened between us was a rare experience. We were so good together. Chelsea, I'm not bragging, but I've known a lot of women. And nothing has ever come even remotely close to what we shared that night."

She was grateful for the darkness, and in fact, wanted to be swallowed by it so he couldn't see the truth swimming in her eyes.

"There's a future for us, Chelsea. Maybe you can't see that right now, but I know there's a future. Don't slam the door in my face. Let me know the real you."

"You won't like the real me."

"I'm willing to risk it."

"I'm not. Logan, our emotions are unimportant right now. I feel guilty that I could think of anything knowing that Daddy is lying on a cold steel table in the morgue while his murderers are running free. And what about Walter? I've got to know what happened to him. Why can't we find him tonight?"

Logan sank back into the seat and rubbed his hand over his whisker-stubbled chin. "No, I'd rather let Dad take care of this. I'll call him first thing in the morning. No sense getting him out of bed in the middle of the night."

"Maybe I'm jumping to conclusions. Maybe Walter is safe with Doralee, but I've got to see him in the flesh before I'll be satisfied."

"Chelsea, we have to wait till morning. And then in the daylight, we run the risk of being followed by those damned reporters. If Walter's whereabouts hits the newspaper or TV, then Rena and Sam will know where he is."

Chelsea blew out a sigh. "When will it all end?"

"There's always tomorrow," he stated.

"Tomorrow? I can't think that far ahead."

Chapter 10

Wee small hours of Wednesday morning

Chelsea finally agreed she was too tired and it was too late to return to the motel. As they entered the cool refuge of the dimly lit kitchen, the red light was twinkling on Logan's answering machine parked on the counter. There were two messages--one from Tom Guthrie stating that Claude Hollander's funeral would be held at two on Wednesday afternoon at the Lucchesi Funeral Home. The second call was from Brew Wilder advising that evidence of splatter marks of human blood had been found in the Redbush kitchen, along with a drag-trail leading to the swimming pool. Brew went on to advise that Sam and Rena had a ten o'clock appointment at police headquarters for another round of questions.

"Does this mean they can file murder charges against Rena and Sam?" Chelsea asked hopefully.

"All the evidence has to be presented to the District Attorney who will decide if it's strong enough to get a conviction," Logan explained.

"What if the DA doesn't move fast enough? If Sam and Rena think the cards are playing against them, they might try to leave town?" she argued.

"They want Hollander money. Unless they get spooked, they'll try to wait it out. Divide to conquer--that's the method homicide investigators use. They'll put them in separate interrogation rooms, then try to pit one against the other. Since Sam probably committed the murder, Rena might be bargained into testifying against him to save herself. It could take hours."

"But, but--"

"Chelsea, you're being too impatient. The wheels of justice don't roll as fast as you'd like them to."

"Well, there is one thing I can do." She dialed information and asked for the number of Doralee Jacobs, but there was none listed. "She probably can't afford a phone."

"Maybe she has a cell phone," Logan commented. "Did Walter have one?"

"I have no idea." Chelsea put her face in her hands.

"You're dead on your feet. Why don't you go upstairs and try to get a few hours' sleep. Everything has to be done in logical order and according to the rules."

"Spit on your rules." Chelsea stomped out to her car to retrieve her cosmetic bag and a change of clothes.

"Last bedroom on the right--the one closest to the bathroom," Logan told her as she recrossed the kitchen. "Frowning doesn't become you," he added as an afterthought, but she was already out of hearing range.

***

Sleep was impossible. Logan's mind galloped through every imaginable emotion, every possible solution concerning

Chelsea and himself. He thrashed about, struggling to find some way to resolve their turbulent relationship. He knew she was feeling something positive by her passionate response to his kisses. So why was she fighting him at every turn? Logan set aside the book he was pretending to read, threw the cover off and strode down the hall in his underpants. The bottoms of his bare feet collected a thin layer of dust coating the hardwood floors. He approached Chelsea's bedroom quietly, wondering if she had been more successful than he in falling asleep.

"Chelsea?" Her name emerged as a question. "You awake?" The bed linens were rumpled, but Chelsea was nowhere in sight. He sprinted down the stairs, into the kitchen and found her filling the coffee maker.

"What are you doing?"

Her glance lingered a few seconds on his bare, muscular chest. "I'm making coffee, then I'm going to go find Walter."

"Now? Dammit, it's only three o'clock. Your dad's funeral is this afternoon."

"I'll be there. After that I'm going back to Jackson. Call me when you convict Daddy's murderers. Call me when you get his estate settled. Sell Redbush, sell every damned picture and every damned stick of furniture. I can't handle this any more."

"Chelsea, I don't understand you."

"Join the club. I don't understand me."

"I thought we agreed not to go to Doralee's apartment

158

right now. We might lead the reporters directly to Walter. Hell, they're camped on our doorstep. It'll make the radio, TV and newspapers by morning." He made wild, exasperated gestures with his hands. "What if Wheeler has an accomplice watching us, somebody mixed in with the reporters? Dad can find the place in the morning. Let him do the checking with a couple of uniformed officers. He can take the entire family into protective custody. You heard Dad on the answer machine. The police ran tests at the house tonight and found evidence of human blood. They killed him. We're close to having enough evidence to convict Sam Wheeler of murder and probably getting Rena as an accessory." He shut his mouth and waited for a response, but none was forthcoming. "You can't leave now."

"Just stand back and watch me." She was fresh from the shower, her hair was damp, with curls clinging to her neck.

"Dammit woman! You're enough to drive a man to drink!" Logan snatched a bottle of vodka from the pantry and a pitcher of orange juice from the fridge. In less than thirty seconds, he had mixed two drinks, shoved one across the kitchen table toward Chelsea and drained his own glass in three very loud gulps.

Chelsea daringly followed suit and slammed the glass back to the table. "I can't handle death, much less murder, besides, nothing I could possibly do will change that--Daddy's dead, he's gone. All the money in the world can't undo what I've done and haven't done; what I've said and all the things I never said but should have. It's something I'll have to live with every bloody day for the rest of my miserable life. Right now, I just want to go back to my dull, boring little existence as a mother and a small town school teacher." Horror over her slip-up tore the breath from her lungs, but Logan was apparently too angry to notice.

He grasped her shoulders and swung her around to face him. "You're acting like a spoiled brat. I thought you were better than that. So it hasn't been easy. Life wasn't meant to be a picnic in the park. It's a daily struggle of right against wrong."

She twisted free of his grip on her shoulders and planted her feet in hostile defiance, fire danced from her vivid purple eyes. "Can't you think of anything original to say?"

"Like 'actions speak louder than words?'" All Logan's anger was channeled into burning desire. He pulled her against his chest, kissed her so hard her lips hurt, then shoved her away. "Maybe I can't come up with anything original, but those clichés fit this situation. Dammit, I'm in love with you, but you aren't an easy person to love. In fact, you're making it downright difficult!"

Shock rifled through her body. No, it wasn't shock, it was passion, pure liquid passion and it scared the hell out of her. He said the word she wanted to hear--love--and it sent a powerful rush of need vibrating through her flesh. All her blood seemed to be pooling between her thighs. She felt such a strong wave of dizziness that she plopped onto the edge of a kitchen chair to keep from falling to the floor.

"There's nothing new under the sun," Logan said. "Every thing's been said, been done. No matter how compelling, how wonderful and unique we think our feelings are, someone else before us has experienced the same thing."

He lifted her into his arms. She lacked the desire to fight him and buried her face in his shoulder as he carried her effortlessly up the stairs to his own room. He dumped her roughly onto the bed and fell on top, pinning her wrists over her head with one massive hand, bracing his weight with the other.

"I'm going to make love to you. I'm going to do what I've been dreaming about for the past eighteen months. Show me your heart, Chelsea. Show me the real you."

One kiss--neither hard nor gentle, both demanding and giving--brought them together as never before. Their lips separated with pained reluctance as they undressed each other. That hefty splash of alcohol dulled the edge of her inhibitions as she wriggled out of her clothes. As before, her exquisite beauty took his breath away--her breasts were perfectly round, her rosy nipples small, hard and erect. Her skin was golden brown, not pale--as though the sun had gently kissed every square inch of her flesh. A dark-complexioned angel with luminescence radiating from within.

The small reading light beside the bed cast Logan's larger-than-life shadow on the wall behind him. Her gaze leisurely scanned the length of his body with obvious hunger. He was bare-chested, wearing only a thin pair of boxer shorts. The fly was gaping open revealing the full power of his excitement. His long, lean body had a light smattering of black, curly hair down the center of his chest. Chelsea was consumed by the desire to lie against him, to feel the tickle of each and every individual hair against her naked breasts as she had done on that night a very long time ago.

She was all he imagined, all he remembered and more. Staggeringly beautiful. "You take my breath away," he whispered. His hand slid beneath her bent knee, glided along her silky thigh to her waist, to her back. He touched her cheek, deeply moved by the trust shining in her eyes, and left completely wordless by the extraordinary power of his response.

All his adult life he had played at love, indulged in sex for the sole purpose of satisfying his own selfish demands. Everything was suddenly changed. It mattered. Chelsea mattered. He wanted to give more than he took.

His tongue was liquid pleasure as he tasted and explored her body--stirring her passions and touching her heart with magic. The brush of his wavy, brown hair against her inner thighs sent her senses swirling. She wasn't a passive recipient--tasting and touching until Logan was nearly out of control. She rearranged their entwined limbs until she could press her hips against his erection--so close and yet so far away. Unyielding with her demands, she tugged to nudge him on top of her. She couldn't wait another second, but wanted him now. Quickly. A heady feeling coursed through her body when he entered her and slid upward to the full depth her smallness would allow. All her thoughts dwelled on his hard presence buried so deeply inside. He was the one person in the world who could touch her soul, who could rescue her from drowning in the deep sea of loneliness and lies. She wanted to savor this wonderful moment of joining. The spirals of pleasure streaked outward flooding her mind and body, washing over her in inundating waves of never-ending pleasure. The mesmerizing intensity of her joy was so great it bordered on physical pain.

She wanted to grasp every ounce of delight, prolong the excitement, let nothing escape until all her longings were satisfied and put to rest. His muscles were rigid from the strain of holding back. The rhythm was feverish, intense and powerful. Only when he brought her to orgasm several successive times, did he allow his own pleasure to explode.

He collapsed on top of her, too winded to move. She wouldn't allow him to withdraw, but held him tight until desire quickened again.

Chapter 11
Wednesday morning

The sun was up, but Logan was snoring softly. It was a reenactment of that Friday morning following her Thanksgiving Day fiasco. Chelsea carefully slipped from his bed, gathered her clothes and tiptoed down the hall completely naked. In the unused bedroom, she hurriedly dressed, gathered her belongings and headed for the kitchen. After splashing cold water on her face, and a hit and a miss with her toothbrush and comb, she left.

To hell with the media, she thought as one mini-van and a dark blue sedan fell in behind her. *Let them follow me now. Let the shit hit the fan before sunset!*

The first order of business was coffee and a quick bite to eat, the second was to buy a city map, and third was finding Walter and Doralee.

Within an hour, she knocked on the door of apartment number six. "Walter, Walter," she whispered hoarsely. When he opened the door, she fell into his open arms. "I've been wild with worry."

"It's all right. I'm okay. Got to admit, Miss Chelsea, I been scared half out of my wits."

She held him at arms' length and studied his aging features to make sure he was okay, then pulled him to the sofa. "Begin at the beginning--last Thursday."

164

"I woke up much earlier than usual that day, about five thirty and headed to the big house to fix breakfast for Mister Claude. Sometimes in the early morning quiet, we'd chat over our coffee and Danish. As I approached the kitchen door, I saw him floating face down in the pool. I waded in, pulled his body to the edge. He was too heavy for me to lift, but I knew, I knew he was already dead. I hollered for help and Sam came outside. We hauled Mister Claude out of the water." Reliving those awful moments was upsetting, but Walter knew that he had to tell her every detail. "I tried to find a pulse--but nothing. I did CPR until I was exhausted--but nothing. I keep thinking that maybe I should have done more."

"No, no, there was nothing else you could have done. The Medical Examiner said Daddy was murdered. He was hit in the head, lost consciousness and then drowned. Did you see Sam hit him with anything?"

"No, Sam told me to wait outside, that he'd go and call the police. But I could see in the big window over the sink and Rena was washing the walls in the kitchen. They didn't call 911 right away either...but took their own sweet time to do it."

"Did they know you could see them through the window?"

"I don't think so, they were so preoccupied. But I can tell you that it was really unusual to see them that early in the morning. They would never get up before nine or ten."

Chelsea ran her fingers through her tousled hair. "Washing didn't help. The police did a chemical test last night and found the blood splatter on the kitchen walls and on the pavement leading to the pool. Sam and Rena probably planned to kill Daddy and get back to bed before you came in at six thirty. What happened next?"

"They finally called 911, then I called Tom Guthrie on the phone extension in the pool house. All hell broke lose. Questions. Detectives everywhere. I didn't know what to do or who to talk to. It seemed to me that Sam and Rena were watching me like hawks. Late Thursday night after I'd gone to bed, I heard sounds of someone trying to break into my house."

"Sam and Rena?"

"I'm almost certain it was them, but there were some real shady characters that came around to see Sam about all those cars he had. I hid in that tiny old storm cellar. You remember, the one under the kitchen pantry floor."

"Oh, I'd forgotten about that. What then?"

"They found my car keys and drove it away. I put on shoes and pants and ran like hell!"

"How did you get here to Doralee's?"

"Walked. I left the house without my wallet. I didn't have a penny to my name, no ID, no credit cards. Nothing."

"Why didn't you call Tom or the police?"

"Miss Chelsea, Doralee doesn't have a phone and we've

both been too scared to leave this apartment."

"Everything is going to be all right now." She patted the old man's hands. "Walter, what happened to Daddy over the last year or so?"

"It was like the life-blood drained out of him after the fight you had at Thanksgiving."

Chelsea didn't need to hear that. "I know," she mumbled. "I should have apologized. I should have, I should have...." She buried her face in her hands.

Walter caringly stroked Chelsea's shoulder. "You can't undo the past, Missy."

Chelsea fought to regain her composure. "You're right. I can't undo words and deeds. Walter, do you think Daddy was physically ill?"

"Miss Rena started your dad on a regimen of pills. She said they were vitamins and herbs and would make him feel young and peppy. They didn't. I've got my own regrets to live with, my own list of things I should have done. It just didn't seem to be my place to doubt Miss Rena's motives. Mister Claude just didn't want to hear anything bad about her. She was doing all she could to push me out. After I fixed breakfast, she would say, 'We won't need you any more today, Walter.'"

"She was trying to fire you? Were you still getting your salary?"

"Mister Claude set up a trust fund for me two years ago,

maybe more. I've been getting an automatic deposit paid by the bank, not by Miss Rena or Sam."

"Well, apparently Daddy had enough presence of mind to protect you." Chelsea paused to wonder why her father had not done the same for her. "Does Sam have a job?"

"Not in the last year. He spent most days in your dad's office on his computer and going over the finances--things that were none of his business. I think he was doing some shady things. Mister Claude would sign anything they stuck under his nose. Before long, Sam started writing the checks for household expenses."

During their conversation, Doralee tried to reign in her two boys' enthusiasm, but it was a fruitless effort. As Chelsea watched the two youngsters crawling all over their great-grandfather, she decided that children really did need grandparents and extended family. Yes, she would have to tell Logan the truth, but until she could get her head screwed on straight, running away was the easiest solution. Chelsea stood up. "Come along. I'm going to drop all four of you off at Tom Guthrie's office. You'll be safe with him."

"Have those two been arrested yet?" Walter asked with fear dulling his eyes.

"The last I heard, they were due to undergo more questions at Police Headquarters this morning. They'll probably be arrested then. Lord, I hope so. Listen, don't be frightened, but I'm being followed."

"Who?"

"Reporters. Walter, they're digging into my past." Chelsea took a few extra minutes and told him about what happened after the Thanksgiving Day fight with her dad; about Logan Wilder; and the birth of her son.

For the first time a happier spark sprang to life in Walter's tired, frightened eyes. "A boy? Oh, I wish the Mister was around to see this baby."

"I wish the reporters would make themselves useful and keep an eye on Sam and Rena instead of me. I've got to buy something to wear to Daddy's funeral. You guys will be safe with Tom. You can attend the funeral with him. I'll see you at two this afternoon."

Chapter 12
Wednesday morning

The slump of Logan's shoulders spoke of fatigue and defeat as he entered the suite of offices on Wednesday morning. Susan felt an immediate twinge of sympathy for him. Although his face was clean-shaven, there were dark shadows beneath his eyes-- something she'd never witnessed before on his normally handsome features. "Good morning, Mister Wilder. Is anything wrong?"

"Everything is wrong," he snapped, then immediately regretted venting his foul temper on the secretary. But on this particular morning, her perpetual good humor rubbed him the wrong way. He halted mid-step. "I'm sorry, Susan. Great night, but a bad morning." Yes, it was a bad morning, he silently mused. He had awakened to find his bed partner missing. Chelsea's continual disappearing acts were grating on his nerves.

Tom Guthrie hobbled into the waiting room as Logan was pouring a cup of coffee.

"Good morning, Mister Guthrie." Susan beamed. "How are you feeling today?"

"Tolerable after my breakfast of pain pills. Only two more weeks and I'll get my new knee."

"We'll be calling you the bionic man," she teased.

"Anything exciting happen overnight?" Tom asked Logan as he poured himself a cup of coffee.

"Yes, in more ways than I can ever tell you." Logan drew in a deep breath and tried to find a bit of calm to ease his turbulent state of mind. "However, down to the business at hand, when I talked to Dad this morning, he told me the Luminal test the criminalists did last night at Redbush came up positive for human blood."

"Wonderful. Is it enough to make an arrest?"

"I don't know yet. Sam and Rena are supposed to go to Police Headquarters this morning for another round of questions. Dad said he'd call me when it's over." Logan patted the cell phone in his pocket, then raked his fingers through his hair. "I don't know if I'm cut out to handle these murder investigations, Tom. It's too damned nerve wracking."

"I don't think that's the problem, my boy. I think you've gotten too personally involved in the outcome of this particular case. I've seen the way you look at Chelsea--all moon-eyed. I wasn't born an old man."

Logan sipped the hot coffee and silently agreed with Tom's off-handed but obviously correct assessment.

"Oh, Mister Guthrie." Susan waved a small square object. "When the new carpet was installed earlier this morning, the workers found this photo under your desk. Whose baby?"

Tom's expression softened visibly. "Logan, look. This is a picture of Cody Hollander, Chelsea's baby. Isn't he a doozy? I can scarcely wait to get my hands on him. There's nothing like sweet baby kisses, isn't that right, Susan?"

The world stopped, or at least the world as Logan thought he knew it stopped rotating and a muddled hum began roaring in his ears. "Chelsea? She, she has a ba-baby?" His trembling hand moved in slow motion as Logan set his coffee on the corner of the secretary's desk and slipped the picture from Guthrie's hand. "Cody Hollander?" He mouthed the unfamiliar name. His voice was slightly muted, but heavy with wonder as he stared at the child's cheery little smile, big brown eyes and dark curly hair. "Ba-baby? This is Chelsea's baby? But, but, who--"

"Didn't she tell you about him?"

"No, she did not," he snapped as anger turned volcanic and began to gain momentum, threatening to erupt.

"I'm surprised. She had a stack of photos this long." Tom gestured broadly.

"Is there a husband, a daddy?" Logan asked, his gaze still glued to the small photo.

"Oh no. Well, of course there was a, a, what-do-you-call-it? A biological father. Yes, but, but no, there isn't a husband," he stammered over the embarrassing subject matter. "She's a single parent and apparently done very well for herself and the child. The girl doesn't have a mercenary bone in her body. She only wants enough of her father's money to insure that Cody has sufficient funds for a proper college education. Such a pity that Claude never had a chance to meet his grandson." Guthrie tapped the photo with his fingertip. "Just look at that handsome face."

"How old is this baby?" Logan was not familiar enough with infants to be able to gauge the age of one, especially in his present state of mental upheaval.

"Under a year. I think she said he's ten months old."

Logan made some quick mental calculations: nine months of pregnancy plus a ten month old baby roughly subtracted out to that fateful Thanksgiving Day encounter. He slowly shook his head from side to side, trying to allow this startling declaration sufficient time to seep into his consciousness and find registration as fact.

"She's going to bring the boy to visit me next week. Since Claude has passed away, I'm his newly appointed grandfather," Tom continued with a touch of pride in his voice. "Goodness gracious, it'll be wonderful to experience all that happy chaos again. Damn, I've been so lonesome since Emily died. I'm going to have to persuade her to move back to Memphis." With a rare burst of raucous laughter, he slapped Logan on the shoulder. "This will be even better than a dog, Logan, my man."

As Tom chattered on, an instant replay of events over the past few days unwound in slow review inside Logan's head-- Chelsea's immediate fear when they first met in Guthrie's office; again when the pictures fell on the floor; plus all the hedging about where she lived and to top it off all the other lies and fabrications she told on every imaginable subject.

The phone call and her declaration of "How's my big fella" and "Yes Cody sweetheart, I love you very much" and "Goodbye, honey, I'll talk to you in a couple of days." And her flimsy explanation, "Cody is...he's someone I know back home. Nothing serious."

Nothing serious? This is damned serious!

Then his thoughts went to the incident in his upstairs hall when Chelsea correctly pointed out his baby picture from the collage of photos of himself and his siblings. The sting of betrayal was close to unbearable. She had conceived his child and then blatantly told a string of lies to hide that fact. He continued to shake his head in renouncement. "No, no," he said aloud, not wanting to believe that Chelsea was capable of such faithlessness.

"I went out with the realtor yesterday afternoon," Tom continued, seemingly unaware of Logan's mounting anguish. "I've found a house I really like. It's damn near perfect for my needs. All on one floor. A great place for me to recuperate from my knee surgery. Got a nice fenced yard, big shade trees, and a roomy apartment over the garage. It's empty, so I can have it as soon as the money is settled. I'd like to get out of that apartment before my surgery. Maybe you and Chelsea can help me move this weekend. By the way, where is she?" Tom asked.

Logan tore his riveted attention from the picture. "I, I haven't the foggiest notion. She slept with me last night, but when I woke up this morning, she was gone from my bed," he said, driven by the sudden prod of anger to lash out at her even in absentia.

Tom choked slightly on his embarrassment as he plopped onto the corner of Susan's desk with his mouth gaped open. "Slept with you? Gone? Where?"

"I told you, I don't know." Logan couldn't get a grip on his rage. "I drove by the Holiday Inn, but she's not there, already checked out."

"Surely she didn't go back to Jackson. Claude's funeral is this afternoon at two o'clock."

"She knows that. We got your message on the answer machine last night." The hand that held the picture was trembling slightly as Logan resumed staring at the glossy photo. The shock of instant fatherhood was overwhelming. Most guys have nine months to adjust to the idea, he'd had fewer than nine minutes. "Son. I have a son. He's my duplicate," he muttered. "My Goddamn duplicate."

"Your son?" Tom's mouth gaped open. "But how on earth did that happen?"

"The same way children have been conceived since the beginning of time." There was a hard edge to Logan's voice as he turned slightly to face the older man a second time. "Do you need instructions on the birds and the bees? On this particular morning, I'm just the man to teach you."

Tom sputtered. "No, but, but that means you've known her longer than-- Oh, I understand it now. You must have been

175

her, her indiscretion."

"Indiscretion? Is that what she called our son and me? Her indiscretion?" When Logan's mind went blank, he fell back on repetition. Father. He was a father. Lies, she told so damned many lies.

"What a wild coincidence."

"Not really. We met in the bar across the street from our old office building the night she was disowned by her father."

"Ooh, no wonder she asked me not to mention Cody to you. I couldn't understand her reasoning at the time, but now I do."

"When was that?"

"At, at dinner on Sunday night."

Susan's head swiveled back and forth as if she were a spectator at a tennis match listening with rapt attention to the heated repartee. As Tom struggled to recover his poise, she finally regained her train of thought. "Oh, Mister Guthrie, I'm so sorry, I almost forgot to tell you. Walter Scruggs and his granddaughter are waiting in your office. He's been safe and sound at her apartment all this while. I know how worried you've been about him."

"Thank God. Come along, Logan, let's question the man."

Logan slipped the photo into his pocket and attempted to redirect his thoughts. "Last night Chelsea and I found Doralee's address."

"How did you find that fortunate bit of information?"

"Don't ask, Tom. Don't ask. I can't believe what I did. I

called Brew early this morning and asked him to take Walter into protective custody as a material witness. But when he got there, the apartment was empty. Apparently Chelsea beat him to it."

Walter Scruggs was every inch the gentleman's gentleman of olden years--tall, slender with graying hair. His eyes were deeply set and filled with a mix of concern and fear.

Tom and Walter embraced as the old friends they were. "Walter, we've been desperate to find you." Tom pulled a small tape recorder from his desk drawer. "Now, tell us what happened."

Chapter 13
Late Wednesday afternoon

From his hidden vantage point, Logan could see that Chelsea was dressed in a trim-fitting black suit as she stood next to her father's coffin listening to a minister who was reading a passage from the Bible. Tom Guthrie stood beside her, leaning heavily on a cane, one arm protectively circling her small waist. Walter Scruggs was on the other side of Chelsea, who in turn was comforting the elderly black man, also stooped by grief.

The many sprays of flowers had been neatly arranged beneath the striped tent, their fragrance overpowering in the afternoon heat.

Logan continued to watch as Chelsea laid a single yellow rose on the closed coffin, then stepped back as it was lowered into the ground. Her normally tanned complexion had a light touch of matte gray, her lips were pale and colorless. Her eyes seemed deeper set, circled with a mantle of sadness. Her proud stance was bent, head and shoulders drooping. For all the world, she appeared completely broken, but that didn't come close to dampening his anger.

As the ceremony drew to a conclusion, Logan approached Chelsea from the rear and grasped her elbow with a strong, unexpected grip. "You're coming with me," he snarled.

Chelsea uttered a startled cry and looked to Tom for help.

Tom shook his head solemnly. "No Chelsea, go with Logan," he urged. "You two have a lot to discuss."

Chelsea reluctantly allowed herself to be led to Logan's silver Mercedes. His grim expression made her stomach churn uneasily. He was almost hurtful in the way he shoved her into the car seat.

"Buckle up," he barked. "God forbid that anything happen to you before I have a chance to chew your ass out."

Too frightened to argue, Chelsea mutely did as she was told. *He knows,* she thought, her mind racing through every other possible scenario. *He knows about Cody.* As he drove, Chelsea's fear and apprehension grew, but she could not summon the courage to open her mouth in protest. Neither spoke a word during the short drive from the cemetery to his house.

He parked in the garage at the rear of his property. Still silent, he pulled her from the vehicle and dragged her into the kitchen. He flung his car keys on the table, shrugged out of his suit jacket, laid it on the kitchen counter and loosened his tie with a savage jerk.

She stood in the middle of the floor wrenching her hands with her gaze locked to the tile floor, its innocence assaulting her senses.

"Sit down," he ordered gruffly and she hurriedly obeyed. Logan tossed the picture of Cody on the table. "Start explaining."

She drew in a slow, deep breath, willing to use anything

179

to stall the inevitable. At least, it was out in the open, she thought, and yet she was still unable or maybe still unwilling to face the subject squarely. "There's nothing to explain," she whispered.

"You gave birth to my child. Doesn't that need explaining?" Logan paced the short distance between the breakfast table and the counter.

"You know how and when it happened as well as I do."

He halted a moment to stare at her. "Yes, I think I do remember that wild night of passion, and might I remind you that what happened between us was one-hundred-percent mutual. We both might have been a trifle tipsy, but it wasn't rape and it wasn't brutality. In fact, it was downright romantic. What I didn't know about was the aftermath of that night. Why didn't you let me know you were pregnant? Why didn't you get in touch with me?"

"I didn't know your name or how to contact you."

"I think you're lying to me again. You knew I graduated from Vanderbilt University in Nashville. Hell, you checked out my class ring when we were in that little bar. You could have matched my picture with my name in the college yearbook. No, I don't buy that feeble excuse. Try again."

"Okay...you're right. That was another lie. I did go to the public library and look up your name. But I decided I wouldn't ask for your help or support."

"May I ask why not?"

"It was my mistake and it was my responsibility to live

with it." Her winsome vulnerability had changed into something hard and ugly.

"Is that what you think every time you look at this child?" Logan stabbed at the photo with one finger. "He's your mistake, your indiscretion?"

"No, no, you're twisting my words."

"I'd like to twist more than your words! I'd like to wring that pretty little neck of yours, and paddle that cute little butt." Logan lifted the empty ladder-back chair a few inches then banged it to the floor to assuage his anger. "What kind of heel do you think I am? Do you think I wouldn't care that I'd fathered this child? That I wouldn't feel a sense of responsibility to him? I'm not some pimple-faced teenager who grabbed a quickie in the back seat of a car. Yes, I guess I let passion get the best of me and I was careless. In fact, we both were careless. Truthfully, I never even thought about using a condom that night and neither did you. Most sexually active women in this day and age take birth control pills. But I'm a man who takes full responsibility for my actions."

"I know that, Logan, and I know you're an honorable man. Tom Guthrie thinks the sun rises and sets on you and rightfully so. But, but I, I thought you might deny knowing me, demand DNA testing, or maybe try to.... Dammit, I didn't know what you might do. It's a moot point and right now I'm too tired and upset to care."

"You want to know what I care about, Chelsea? I care about all the lies you've told me. My God, they've slipped from

181

your lips like honey in the July sun. I never met anyone who could tell so many lies with such a straight face. You even convinced poor old Tom Guthrie to lie for you. That's rotten."

The anger shrouding his words tore into her heart and ripped it to tiny pieces. It was so obvious to her now, her love for Logan. A love that began the night when Cody was conceived and had grown and flourished despite neglect, separation and denial. She sighed with grim resignation. There would be no salvation of this relationship. It was doomed, and its demise was firmly lodged on her shoulders. All she wanted right now was to crawl into a small hole, pull the door shut behind her and wait until the raw edges of her wounds had healed. She hung her head in defeat. "I told you that if you ever got to know the real me, that you wouldn't like what you found."

"What I told you that night is...that I wanted to see your heart. Is this the real you, Chelsea? The way you're acting right now? Or is this another wall you've built? Another wall of lies."

"You, you backed me into a corner. I had to lie to protect Cody."

"Protect him from what? Me? Am I some fearful bastard? What do you plan on telling our son when he's about eight years old and he asks who his daddy is?"

"Don't preach to me. You sound too much like Mandy."

"Somebody needs to preach to you with a little hell fire and damnation. I'd hate to be in your shoes when my mother gets a hold of you. She's a formidable woman and put the fear of God into us kids when we were growing up." Logan dropped wearily into the chair opposite Chelsea, bowed his head and rubbed at his temples with his fingertips as though trying to thwart a headache. When he spoke again, his voice was soft as if his emotions had jumped from rage to the opposite end of the spectrum. "I fell in love with you that night, Chelsea. Yeah. Big city lawyer knocked on his ass in a one-night-stand." He picked up Cody's picture and stared intently, slowly taking in each of his tiny features. "I don't need DNA testing. Look at him. This kid is definitely mine. I don't have an ounce of doubt. He looks just like my baby pictures. My mom will flip."

His declaration of love, although in the past tense, launched the water works, and the tears channeled down her cheeks. "I didn't think you'd believe me. Can't you understand? I didn't think you'd believe me."

Logan reached across the table and grasped Chelsea's primly folded hands. "Look at me. You may be lying with words, but your body can't lie. You cannot fake your undeniable physical response every time we've touched and every time I've kissed you. And last night? The fire, the passion? Was that all a lie, a sham?"

"Logan, please. Put yourself in my place and try to understand this situation from my perspective. Everything happened at once. Daddy disowned me, took away my car, my insurance, cut off all my money, and then I turned up pregnant. I was nearly penniless and very much alone, not to mention afraid of losing my job. I was only in the second year of my teaching contract. I spent many sleepless, soul-searching nights coming to terms with my predicament. Abortion didn't seem to be an option for me."

"Thank God for that."

"I knew I wanted this baby." She slowly lifted her tearful gaze and met Logan's steady stare. "Your baby," she whispered softly. "Yes, I agree with you...that night was a poignant coming together of two lonely people. I'll admit I probably could have found you, but then what? Knock on your door and say, 'Hey, guess what? Do you remember that night we spent at the Holiday Inn? Well, I'm pregnant and I need a few hundred bucks to help pay the doctor bills!' You would have probably laughed and slammed the door in my face. No, I've got too much pride for that. My damnable pride has always been my main screw-up."

"I don't know how I would have reacted initially, but you never gave me the chance to find out. We're not leaving this kitchen, Chelsea, until we come to a complete understanding. I want to know my son. I want to be a father to him. And the law is on my side."

"You probably won't believe me, given my track record, but once Daddy was buried, and his murderers were behind bars, then...then, once the dust settled, I was going to tell you about Cody. This is the truth. When I met your dad at the Forensic

184

Center, I realized that it wasn't fair to keep Cody isolated from his grandparents. And then this morning when I saw Walter's great-grandchildren crawling into his lap and him hugging them, well, I knew then what I had to do. I grew up without any extended family--my mother was from Italy, my father was an orphan--so I know firsthand how lonely it can be to have no aunts, uncles or cousins. I don't want that sort of life for Cody."

Chelsea laid her face down on folded arms to avoid the pained expression on Logan's face. The gentle touch of his fingers toying with her hair was nearly her undoing. She began choking on the deluge of confessions begging to be unshackled.

"I'm not trying to push you into anything right now," Logan said softly. "Just give us a chance, Chelsea. Give us a chance to get to know each other under less stressful circumstances."

Several things happened in measured sequence. First, the phone rang. Then, as Logan slowly rose from the chair, turned his back to fish the cell phone from his jacket pocket and answer the call, Chelsea looked up. It was a fleeting opportunity. She carefully closed her fingers around his car keys to silence any possible sounds and calmly tiptoed through the kitchen door. A charge of "grand-theft-auto" would be the least of her worries, she rationalized as she hurriedly backed the Mercedes out of the garage.

Escape to home. Escape to Cody. They were the

dominating thoughts occupying every cell of her brain. Neither thoughts of Logan, nor their second remarkable night together, nor even the slim possibility of a future together could make headway into her morass of emotions. Later. Later she would deal with Logan's wishes to become an involved father. Her own father was buried and Walter's testimony--although not an eyewitness to the murder--was nonetheless damning. Even as she was making her getaway, Sam and Rena were probably already under arrest and in jail. The entire matter would be winding down. She was no longer needed in Memphis, but Cody needed her and she missed him beyond all reason. She would worry about Logan later. There was always later.

The look of sad devastation in Logan's eyes would haunt her dreams for a long time to come. She had successfully executed a first-class hatchet job on her life. Logan would never find it in his heart to forgive her. She wouldn't fight him if he asked for visitation rights and certainly couldn't blame him if he washed his hands of her.

Logan was talking to his dad when he heard the big engine of his car roar to life. After a few hurried instructions to Brew, he was quickly on her tail. He knew exactly where she was going. Chelsea's car was parked at the funeral home. After the services, she had ridden to the cemetery with Tom, Walter and Doralee in the provided black limousine. With the aid of his police siren, Brew would get there before she slipped through their fingers again.

Brewster Wilder was leaning against her small white Chevy as she pulled into the parking lot. Were it not for his white hair, Chelsea would have mistaken him for Logan from a distance with his arms folded across his chest in that now familiar stance. His police care barricaded her Chevy. She slowly emerged from the Mercedes and dropped the car keys into his outstretched hand. "I guess I'm under arrest."

"I don't think my son is going to press charges because you 'borrowed' his car. But I've got some very bad news for you, my dear. Very bad."

"Bad news?" Chelsea's scattered attention reluctantly coalesced, drawn to the sound of another vehicle entering the parking lot. It was Logan in his old rattling pickup truck. She refused to meet his gaze as he approached, switching her concern back to the Lieutenant. "What? What sort of bad news?"

"Have you told her yet?" Logan asked his father.

"No, I thought it might be best if it came from you."

"Tell me what? What's going on?" Chelsea demanded.

Logan grabbed Chelsea's shoulders and pulled her around to face him, his fingers digging painfully into her flesh. "There's no easy way to say this. No way to soften the blow. Our son has been kidnapped. Rena and Sam didn't show up for questioning this morning. They left Redbush, drove to Jackson and broke into your house. The thought is that they planned to hide out there until you

187

returned from the funeral, maybe to kidnap, rob or maybe even murder you. The police don't know their exact motives as yet. They can only guess. Possibly when they saw the baby pictures and baby furniture, they changed their plans. According to Amanda Foster, when she went to your house to feed your cat, they pulled a gun and forced her take them to Cody. While we were at the funeral, Sam Wheeler called Guthrie's secretary with a ransom demand. They've asked for a million dollars for the return of the child and for safe passage into Mexico."

Chelsea felt the scalding terror slowly expand throughout her body, then suddenly explode within the tight confines of her brain. This weighty straw was more than her fragile state of mind could handle, and as her knees began to buckle, Logan swept her into his arms and carried her to his Mercedes. "I'll come back for the truck later," he told his dad.

***

Distant sounds pulled Chelsea into a condition of semi-awareness. For a fleeting instant, she didn't know where she was and had momentarily forgotten what had pushed her into this welcomed oblivion. But the truth was there and sliced into her consciousness. She opened her eyes to survey her surroundings and found herself lying on Logan's king-sized bed. The mingled odors of sex, perfume and aftershave from the previous night still lingered on the rumpled sheets. She could only hazily recall the trip from the funeral home's parking lot to the house, except that she was safe in Logan's arms as he carried her up the stairs and gently put her to bed.

Logan was sitting in a bedside chair staring at her across the dimly lit room. He had changed from his suit into jeans and a cotton denim shirt. His face seemed frozen and emotionless, his eyes unreadable, skin stretched too tightly over his cheekbones. She could no longer hide behind Tom or her wall of guilt; she would have to step forward and not only face Logan's painfully truthful accusations, but also the terrifying chain of events that lead to the abduction of her son.

"You okay?" he asked. The softness in his voice belied his hard exterior.

She nodded as she swung her feet over the edge of the bed and attempted to straighten the wrinkles in her black suit. "Do you mind telling me again exactly what happened?" Widely spaced fingers combed through her tousled hair.

"Apparently, Sam and Rena felt the police were closing in on them, so they changed their plans, decided not to go to police headquarters for any more questions. Instead, they cleaned out Redbush of every thing valuable and went to your house in Jackson." Logan reiterated the remainder of the story of Mandy's and Ellen's frightening ordeal.

"Oh no, don't tell me they were dragged into this mess."

"At gun point. Sam tied them up and covered their mouths

with duct tape."

"No, no."

"But that's not the end of it," Logan continued and told her about the phone call demanding a ransom. "Sam and Rena also want safe passage to Mexico."

"A million in cash? How will I ever get that much money?"

"It won't come down to that. Kidnapping is a federal offense and the feds don't give in to ransom demands."

"But Cody! My baby!"

Logan scooted to the edge of the chair. "Correction, Chelsea. Our baby. Our son. The police have set up the phones downstairs with all their electronic equipment. They'll trace the next call that comes in."

"How will Sam know to call here?"

"Susan is going to stay at the office until he calls again. She'll give him this number as the new way to contact you." Logan unfolded his tall frame and stretched his back. "Why don't you pull yourself together and come downstairs."

"Logan?" she whispered as he headed for the door.

The pleading tone coloring her voice caused him to turn and face her with one heavy black brow arched hopefully. Her small hands were gripped into prayerful pose.

"When...when this is over...we'll talk."

"Yeah, we'll talk."

"I promise. I promise I'll tell you everything. Trust me, please trust me."

Logan's expression mellowed even more as she laid her right hand over her heart like a tiny girl scout reciting the Pledge of Allegiance. He returned to Chelsea's side and lifted her from the bed. His strong arms enfolded her in his embrace. For a moment, she felt completely safe from all harm and from the realities of the hurting world, but the feeling only lasted a few brief seconds. Her shoulders began to tremble as she sobbed.

"We'll get him back," he mumbled into her tousled curls. "Even if we have to move heaven and earth, we'll get our baby back."

***

The main floor of Logan's home was in bedlam with the trappings of an old-fashioned wake. Walter and Doralee were busy serving the food brought by caterers and friends. Tom Guthrie, Will Jameson, Logan's parents, sister and married brother, Jerry Bruce--her dad's former foreman, and so many other familiar and not-so-familiar faces were streaming in the door. Introductions and condolences became blurred. This is how life had been at Redbush while she was growing up. Beautifully busy. Doralee's two boys and Logan's two nephews were running through the house, laughing and giggling.

Sharon Wilder, Logan's mother, pulled her aside. She was

an attractive woman, tall, willowy and elegant, and as imposing as her son painted her. "We've been praying very hard, my dear. We'll get that baby, then we'll talk it out between us girls, okay?"

Chelsea could do no more than nod. She thought she had her emotions under control, but dissolved sobbing into the woman's willing arms. Prayer? She hadn't prayed since she was thirteen years old and had asked God to make her mother well. When her mother died, her faith had died as well. Could it ever be resurrected?

Another commotion drew Chelsea's curious gaze to the front door--Mandy and her mother, Ellen Foster, had just arrived from Jackson. Chelsea ran to greet them, gathering them both in one expansive hug. "Ohmygod, Mandy, they threatened you guys with a gun and tied you up. I never dreamed it would come down to such a confrontation. Money, all they want is Daddy's cursed money. I never imagined they would find out where I lived. I tried so hard to keep it a secret." Chelsea babbled as more tears streamed down her cheeks from her red, puffy eyes.

"Hush, hush. It's over and hey, we kept a cool head and survived. But Mom's a basket case for having to hand over Cody to that awful man."

Chelsea pulled them to the sofa and she, Logan and the Lieutenant spent the next thirty minutes reassuring Ellen that she did the right thing. Otherwise, Wheeler might have killed them all--including Cody.

"You did great," Brew tried to reassure them. "Folks trying to elude the cops can get a little desperate."

Tom interrupted them. "Just got a call from Susan on my cell phone. The bank manager just heard about Rena Hollander on his car radio. He said she came into the bank yesterday afternoon and apparently cleaned out the safety deposit box. He said she left with a hefty-sized canvas bag." Tom turned his attention to Chelsea. "Do you have any idea what was in the bank vault?"

Chelsea shrugged helplessly. "It's been so long I'm not sure. After Momma died, Daddy put all her jewelry away. He also had some rare coins, some loose gemstones, and I'm not sure where he kept his collection of antique pocketknives. There was also an Italian crafted letter opener encrusted with diamonds, rubies and emeralds. It was so gaudy, it looked fake."

"By the way, Chelsea," Brew interrupted. "I forgot to tell you that we did uncover one other bit of good news this morning. Sam Wheeler and Rena Allen Wheeler are husband and wife, not brother and sister. Her marriage to your father was not legal. And that leaves you in the clear for an inheritance. Apparently, the marriage was nothing more than a con from the very beginning."

"I'm beginning to believe that Daddy's money is cursed," she whispered. The heavy burden of her guilt seemed to get heavier instead of lighter. If she had stayed in Memphis and not been so damned anxious to get out on her own, her father would not have fallen victim to a fortune hunter. Claude Hollander had

193

known many nice ladies since the death of his wife, Claire. The blame for his loneliness lay squarely on Chelsea's rebellious teenage shoulders. In her eyes, no one could take her mother's place, nor did she want to share her father's attention with another woman. In retrospect, her selfishness was inexcusable. Now, in a tortuous turn of events, the sum total of her actions had led directly to her father's death and the kidnapping of her son. It was a burden that threatened to irreparably break her spirit.

Moments later, when the phone rang, an instant hush fell over the entire group of thirty or more people. Brew and another detective turned on the monitoring equipment set up on the coffee table in the living room of Logan's home. "Stall him as long as you can," Brew instructed. "It takes a few minutes to do the trace."

"It's only eight o'clock. I'll need at least fourteen hours," Chelsea explained to Sam, trying to keep her voice from revealing the true state of her feelings. "I can't get into Daddy's bank until tomorrow morning at ten. They're closed."

"You withdraw one million dollars. Cash. Nothin' bigger than a hundred. I know how much cash is in them bank accounts, so no funny stuff. An' no police," he stated, probably knowing that the call was being recorded and traced. "Arkabutler. You know where I'm talkin' about?"

"Yes. I remember it from when I was a kid."

"Put the money there inside the cabin by noon tomorrow. No later than one o'clock. Then leave."

"Where should I go?"

"Go back to the main highway, check into a motel. After I have a look-see an' count it, I'll tell you where I've left your kid. If I even smell a cop, the deal's off, an' you don't get your kid back. We've sort of taken a shine to him. Understand?"

"Yes, yes, but what about Cody? Is he okay?"

"Yeah, he's fine. Rena's takin' good care a him. I won't call you again until after I get the money. Understand?"

"Yes, yes, but how?"

"You gotta cell phone?"

Chelsea looked to Logan who was nodding. "Yes, I can borrow one."

"Give me the number." After receiving the number, Sam broke the connection.

"The conversation wasn't long enough to pinpoint the exact location, but it originated in Mississippi." Brew rose from the sofa shaking his head. "Chelsea, what can you tell us about this Arkabutler place? I know it's a dam and recreation area down in Mississippi, but what are you supposed to remember?"

She slipped from the sofa onto the floor and buried her face in her hands. "Later, later. Let me collect my thoughts first."

"No, we have to move quickly to formulate a plan."

"Daddy owned property there, a summer cottage. I can't remember exactly where it is. It's, it's been too long. I was just a kid. Ask Walter, ask Tom, maybe they can tell you about it." A plan of her own was already taking shape in her weary mind. She dried her tears and looked up to Logan with a plaintive expression. "Where's my car? I need some personal items."

"A deputy brought it. It's parked on the street out in front."

"May I get my luggage and a change of clothes?" she asked in a submissive tone. "I'd like to take a shower and put on something more comfortable than this suit and high heels."

"The keys are on the hall table," he responded. "You do look beat. Why not take a few minutes to rest. It's up to the police from here on. We can't do anything right now."

***

Chelsea returned to the living room an hour later freshly showered and dressed in dark cotton knit slacks, a matching tee shirt and sandals. In the confusion of people arriving and leaving, no one was paying close attention to her comings and goings. A smile here, a hug there, and many words of comfort. To avoid undue attention, she didn't carry her purse; rather she had hidden her wallet under a sofa pillow and the car keys were stuffed into her bra.

Considering the short length of time, Walter, Doralee and the caterers had managed to set up an impressive buffet in Logan's dining room. She picked at the food and appeared as calm and restrained as was possible under the burden of events over the past week, and especially after learning of the kidnapping of her infant son. In actuality, she was numb.

Lieutenant Wilder had reassured her numerous times that Sam and Rena would be captured and Cody would be safely returned. There was absolutely nothing she could do--except wait. Even though the ransom demand would not be met, they had to allow Wheeler to think it would be. She would make the fake drop at the appointed time, and the police would arrest Sam. However, the lack of action over the next twelve hours grated on Chelsea's nerves. She wanted something done, and wanted it done now. She pulled Tom away from the group.

"Tom, what about the money? Does Daddy have that much cash you can put your hands on?"

"Sam seems to think there's that much in the various bank accounts, but we have no idea what they were doing with the other assets without Claude's knowledge." Tom shook his head sadly. "Poor Claude, he seemed so confused the last time I talked to him. Sort of remote and sleepy eyed."

"If Rena cleaned out the safety deposit box, why didn't she clean out the bank account before they left Memphis?"

"Listen to me, sweetheart, neither you nor Rena can march into the bank and withdraw one million dollars. I doubt if they keep that much cash on hand. Even though Rena wasn't your father's legal wife, we're still going to have to endure some court procedures to get the mess straightened out and have you named

197

the legal beneficiary. Besides, neither the local police nor the FBI is going to give in to any financial demands. That's not the way they operate."

"I've got to get my baby back safely."

Tom patted her clenched fists. "Take it easy. Let the police handle this matter their way."

***

It had been surprisingly easy to slip away from the house once the sun had gone down and night had closed in around them. Concentrating so heavily on her destination, she wasn't aware of the dark blue sedan that had fallen in behind her. Chelsea knew exactly where the Arkabutler Dam and recreation area was located. She even knew the back road. Her father owned a tiny cabin and small plot of land. When growing up, the lake had been a favorite swimming hole during the long hot days of July. It was a place to see boys and be seen by them. These days, however, it was rented out to tourists during the summer vacation season. In the last ten years, it had been forgotten, neatly wiped from her memory by the pressures of college, career and unplanned motherhood.

She would do this her way, not the police way. Cody was, after all, her son.

Chapter 14
Wednesday night

"Dammit to hell! Has any one seen Chelsea?" Logan roared as he flew down the steps from the second floor.

"She went upstairs to take a shower about an hour ago," Walter commented. "I haven't seen her since then."

"I saw her at the buffet about thirty minutes ago," Mandy offered. "Oh geez, don't tell me Chessie has done another one of her disappearing acts."

"Can you believe it? Dammit, she's gone! Again! How dumb can I be not to have seen it coming?" Logan's anger exploded into violence as he rammed his fist into the nearest wall. "Trust me, she said. And I was fool enough to believe her."

"Surely she wouldn't do such a thing. She wouldn't put Cody's life in jeopardy, or her own." Tom struggled to lift himself from the sagging comfort of the sofa cushions, but in his heart he knew that Chelsea was indeed capable of doing something wildly irrational to regain possession of her child. "Of course, she knew that Sam's ransom demands would not be met. She might...oh dear me."

Logan stepped outside on the front porch and peered into the night to look for her car. "Nope, she's gone. Dammit, she needs her neck wrung for this little trick. Tom, do you know what Sam was talking about concerning the Arkabutler Recreation area?"

"If my memory serves me correctly, Claude owned a cabin and a small parcel of land next to the lake. I don't know exactly where it's located, but we might find a copy of the deed in my old files. It would be somewhere in those boxes we stored in the attic."

"Yes, but how could Sam know about the land?"

"I can answer that question," Walter interrupted Logan. "During the last year, Sam spent a lot of time in Mister Claude's office on his computer, going over his files and finances. The Mister had a whole drawer filled with deeds and legal papers. Even though Mister Claude seemed confused, he did mention something about signing papers so most of the parcels of worthless property could be sold and the profits pooled into other investments. In truth, it could have amounted to a great deal of money."

"Yes, they were probably nickel-diming him into the poorhouse," Logan exclaimed angrily. "Dad, what should we do?"

Brew scowled and shook his head. "Dammit! This little trick is going to force us into action quicker than we want. It's after hours, so we can't get anything from the County Registrar of Deeds down in Mississippi. I guess we'll have to go out to Hollander's house and see what we can find in his files."

"Tom, Walter, you two stay here in case the phone rings. Dad and I will go to Redbush."

"No, you're not leaving me behind," Tom insisted. "You'll need me to read the plats. Don't forget--Chelsea and Cody are the closest things I've got to kin."

***

Logan wanted to see the inside of Redbush, but his concentration was centered on finding Chelsea and Cody, not enjoying fifty-year-old architecture.

In route to the estate, Brew brought his son up-to-date on what had transpired earlier in the day. "When Sam and Rena failed to show up for their appointment, I sort of figured they went missing. I hurried up, got an arrest warrant, and went to Redbush to deliver it in person."

"What time?" Logan asked.

"They were due to come in around nine, and it was noon when we got there to serve the papers. They didn't even bother to lock the front door. All the cars were gone, but according to Mandy and Mrs. Foster, they're driving the silver Rolls Royce."

"Not exactly low profile."

"They left the place in a mess, probably took every thing of value that could be stuffed into the vehicle. Maybe Walter can give us a list of what's missing. I'm certain there's an inventory somewhere that was used for insurance purposes. I left a deputy to guard the place. Thieves are reading the obituaries and robbing houses while folks are attending funerals. According to police records from Mississippi, that's what Sam Wheeler was convicted of down there."

"How come he's on the loose?"

"A screw-up with paper work. It happens too often these days."

"Screw-ups and lies. Screw-ups and lies. Chelsea is just as guilty as they are," Logan stated with disgust. "I can't believe she ran off. What the hell is she up to?"

"No, Logan, you can't place all the blame on Chelsea," Tom argued. "Everyone on the face of this earth is a product of combinations: their upbringing, their environment, even their parents' mistakes. Yes, Chelsea was spoiled as a youngster, but you can blame Claude and Claire for that, not Chelsea. Even though she was spoiled, she rose above it, was a straight-A student in college, graduated with honors. She's also got a healthy dose of pride. And while you might not want to believe it--Claude could be even more implacable and hotheaded than his daughter. Yes, right now you're eaten up with anger because you didn't know about the boy, and I can understand your feelings as well."

"Can you, Tom? Can you know the anguish of being lied to repeatedly by someone you thought you loved?"

"At heart, Chelsea is an honest person, and I think that eventually she would have seen the error of keeping you in the dark about Cody and rectified it."

"It's hard to be logical right now." Logan squeezed his eyes closed. He was a grown man fighting childish tears with every ounce of manly strength he could muster. "If anything happens to

Cody," he whispered. "I don't think I'll ever find it in my heart to forgive her."

"You're wrong, Logan. Dead wrong. You're letting emotions get in the way of reason."

Logan lapsed into a brooding silence as his father maneuvered the police cruiser through heavy Memphis traffic.

The inside of the Redbush house was indeed beautiful with high ceilings, crown molding and expensive, exotic wood trim everywhere. The chandeliers were crystal, the carpets thick, and the furnishings quietly elegant.

It took Logan, Brew and Tom about thirty minutes of hurried and intense searching to find Claude's legal papers concerning the properties Hollander owned.

"Here it is," Tom exclaimed happily. "Plat forty-two, lot six." The old man turned the diagram in several directions. "Let's see, I think this is north, but don't know how we're going to figure out exactly which cabin is theirs in the dark."

"I'll get on the horn to the cops in Mississippi. We'll have to work with them when we cross the State line anyway."

Chapter 15
Late Wednesday night
Mississippi

Rena Allen Wheeler had never given birth to a child. She'd had an abortion once, and thoughts of what that baby might have been like sometimes haunted her dreams. Cody was a living doll. So warm, sweet and good-natured. The child had cried when Sam ripped him from Ellen Foster's arms, but when she had rocked the boy, he eventually quieted and snuggled next to her breasts. She experienced a wave of motherly contentment she'd never known existed. Better even than the kick from drugs or alcohol.

Sam had made two stops after leaving Jackson. One to make a phone call to Tom Guthrie's office about three in the afternoon, and another after dark to talk to Chelsea about eight o'clock.

Before reaching the cabin, Rena made Sam stop a third time at a Super K-mart where she filled a shopping cart with jars of baby food, milk, bottles, diapers, two frozen pizzas and a six-pack of beer. She even bought a diaper bag. She would worry about kid clothes later. Maybe Sam was willing to give up the child for money, Rena was not.

In fact, Rena was already making mental plans to get rid of Sam--permanently. She was tired of his physical and verbal abuse. This morning's argument over whether or not to leave

Redbush resulted in a few additional bruises. Just she and this baby could disappear from sight much easier than with Sam. He wanted high living, whereas she'd be happy to go back home to her mother. It would be easy to pass the kid off as her own. After all, she'd been gone for three years.

"You're bein' awful quiet," Sam commented as he approached the vacation cabin. "Ain't like you not to be runnin' your mouth."

"Don't want to wake the baby," she whispered back.

The elegant car crunched over the gravel road, its precision suspension system swallowing the deep bumps. The Rolls Royce--this rolling billboard of a car--had been another source of argument. It certainly wouldn't blend into the scenery. Rena wanted to take the Jeep--it would hold more, but no, Sam wanted to drive the Rolls. Rena's tongue flicked to the corner of her mouth to explore the newest tear in her flesh inflicted by Sam's violent temper. That was the last blow she was going to endure.

"You go inside," he ordered. "There's 'lectricity, so turn on the lights an' the air conditioning. I gotta find a place to stash this car."

"Are we gonna be safe at this place?"

"We'll have to be outta the cabin before dawn, but we gotta hang around in the woods to wait for the money."

"With this baby, in this heat?"

"You and the kid can wait in the car. I'm goin' to hide it

now."

The furnishings were better than Rena expected. In the not-too-distant past, lack of money had forced her to endure far worse. She carefully placed the sleeping baby on the sofa and wedged a pillow to keep him from tumbling off. While keeping a watchful eye on Cody, she began unpacking the milk, baby food and diapers that she had purchased. If Sam was hungry, he could heat up the pizza. Taking good care of the baby was her job. That...and biding her time. She placed her purse at Cody's feet and unhooked the latch. The gleaming, jewel-encrusted letter opener sat nestled within the darkness of her leather handbag. Ready and waiting.

Funny how gold turns warm in my hand, she thought as her fingers closed around the gem-filled handle. The blade was about ten inches in length. Plenty long enough to slip between Sam's ribs and punch a hole in his cold heart. She'd worked in the trauma unit of the hospital for six months and knew exactly where to strike and fatally pierce that vital organ. Of course, she would have to catch him asleep or off guard because he was carrying a pistol tucked in the waistband of his jeans.

Sex. Maybe she could use sex to tempt him to strip down. It would be his last piece of tail.

Rena had a heavy decision to make: should she wait for the money to be delivered, or get out now? The Rolls Royce could rot in hell. She planned to walk out of the park area--just her, the baby and her purse. There were enough loose gemstones and cash stashed in the bottom of her large pocketbook to buy a beat-up used car and drive to her mamma's place where she could disappear permanently.

Sam didn't know that she had been regularly sending money to a bank down in Wayne County, Mississippi, where her mamma lived. Waynesboro was so far back in the sticks, no one would ever find her. She would get a job, find someone to forge a birth certificate, and settle into life as a single mother. A hundred grand will buy a lot of milk and diapers.

Chapter 16
Late Wednesday night
Sardis, Mississippi

Any hope of light was obliterated by storm clouds covering the moon. Unable to pick out the landmarks in the intense darkness, Chelsea made several wrong turns before finally arriving at the cut-off that led to the cluster of cabins. She parked her car behind some overgrown bushes and cautiously headed out on foot in what she hoped was the right direction. The combination of high temperature and humidity were stifling. Heat lightning arched across the sky with an ominous threat of rain. Wind rustled the leaves in the treetops. Thunder rumbled in the distance. Night creatures blared their raucous calling. The soft sounds of breaking twigs beneath each footfall were all but drowned by the cacophony.

"Which one? Dammit! Which one?" she mumbled. "All the units look alike." The cabins had seemed so much larger in her scattered teenage memories. There would be electricity, she reasoned, since it was used as rental property. Obviously, Sam knew there were no tenants or he would not have suggested it as a drop point. There was a "for sale" sign in front of one of the cottages. The dirt was still fresh where it had been buried. "That must be it."

According to information from Walter, Sam had been

selling off most of her father's smaller properties piece by piece. It was still a source of wonderment to Chelsea that Sam Wheeler had the patience and intelligence to devise such a complicated plan that had taken more than two years to implement.

"What the hell do you think you're doing here, girl?"

Startled, Chelsea uttered a high-pitched squeal and sagged against the jagged trunk of a pine tree. "Who, who are you?"

"Terry Hodges, one of the pesky reporters who's been dogging your ass for the past few days."

Chelsea squinted into the darkness. "You were at the funeral, weren't you?"

"Yeah, I was there."

"I had a creepy feeling I was being watched. Logan said it was the media."

"And I thought I was being so careful. When I saw you sneak from the house tonight, I figured out what happened. I wasn't born fifty years old, girl, I'm a mother too."

"You know I have a baby?"

"Yeah, 'father: unknown' it says on his birth certificate, but I'll bet that's a lie. You don't look like the type to sleep around with a lot of guys."

"You've seen Cody's birth--"

"Of course. I'm part detective and part news hound--it's a great combination."

"If you're such a great detective, what else do you know?"

"I know your baby has been kidnapped and that the police won't give in to the ransom demands," Terry explained.

Chelsea buried her face in her hands and tried to stay composed. "I'm afraid they'll botch everything and something will happen to Cody."

"We're not going to let that happen, are we, girl?"

"My name is Chelsea, not girl."

"Don't get so touchy. I know just about everything there is to know about you."

Chelsea studied the woman as best she could in the darkness, searching for a reason to trust her. Terry Hodges appeared to be middle-aged, dressed in a polyester suit, wearing hose and heavy, cloddy-looking shoes. Her pleasant, angular face was etched in deep lines caused by years of smoking. "But I don't know anything about you."

Terry put her arm around Chelsea's shoulders and squeezed. "Yeah, I want the story, but the older I get, the more I find myself getting too involved with victims, you know, all mushy. Right now, your kid is more important than the story."

"How did you figure this out?"

Terry patted her pockets, searching for a pack of cigarettes. "Honey, I've been chasing down murderers, kidnappers, con artists and alien babies for twenty-five years. This case is fairly classic, but has more twists than a pretzel. Give me some more background info about your dad and his trophy wife."

"The police say it was a con from the beginning, that Rena married Daddy for his money and planned all along to kill him. The police also found out that her marriage to Daddy is null and void because Sam Wheeler is actually Rena's husband, not her brother."

"Wow, gimme an exclusive on that, sweetie, and I should be able to retire sooner than expected." Sensing Chelsea's agitation, Terry patted her knee. "Look, you're not the first to have her mom or dad scammed this way and you won't be the last. This ploy is older than sin. The usual method is to cut the victim off from all family and friends. Make him or her feel isolated."

"You're right. That's exactly what they did."

"This case is a little different, 'cause it's usually widows that get scammed by handsome dudes playing on their vulnerability. Did they use drugs?"

"The autopsy and investigation prove he was murdered, but the blood toxicology report hasn't come back. The police did find a bunch of pill bottles."

"Toxicology tests take forever. But the killers probably used something harmless, but when combined with prescription medicine can leave a fella with a fuzzy brain."

"Damn, how do you know all this?"

"It's my job. The first thing you gotta do is explain to me why this Sam and Rena think they're safe here."

"Apparently, Sam has familiarized himself with all of

Daddy's holdings. We hadn't used this place since I was a teenager. Maybe ten or more years ago. A nearly forgotten asset. Daddy owned a great deal of property scattered all over west Tennessee, eastern Arkansas and northern Mississippi. Oh, Terry, I can't make sense out of all this unless they think that Cody is enough leverage to protect them."

"Yep, they're definitely using that baby as a hostage."

"They want a million dollars cash and safe passage to Mexico. Sam also said that he and Rena had taken a shine to Cody, and if he smelled a cop, I'd never get my baby back."

"You don't have a gun, do you?"

"No."

"Didn't think so, but they oughtta be standard issue for school teachers these days. Hey, that's okay." She patted the area beneath her left arm with a confident smile. "I got my trusty little hand gun."

"You're licensed to carry a concealed weapon?"

"Yep, I'm a licensed private detective, but I think I'm getting too old for this kind of action." Terry slid to the ground beside Chelsea and nervously fingered an unlit cigarette. "So, you're supposed to place the money in the cabin, then leave. They'll call you on the cell phone to tell you where your kid is stashed."

"Yes, yes, that's right. Except, I left in such a hurry that I forgot to bring the phone. But, I still don't understand how you know all this." Even in the darkness, Chelsea could see Terry flash a bright toothy smile.

"I went into the house with the caterers, messed around in the kitchen and stuck a bug under the coffee table. Yeah, I know it's illegal. By the way, your attorney friend, Logan Wilder, is pretty pissed about you leaving unannounced."

"He was angry with me long before I left the house. He found out that he's Cody's father."

"Yeow!" Terry slapped her hand over her mouth to quell her excitement. "I want this entire story, girl. Tabloids will pay top dollar for a story like this."

Chelsea winced at that idea. If her indiscretions were plastered all over the country, she could forget about teaching school anywhere. "You work for the tabloids?"

"Nope, I'm freelance. But we'll talk about that later."

"It was an accident that Sam and Rena found Cody. They went to my house looking for something to steal, and then Mandy showed up to feed my cat."

"A comedy of errors, but then that's what life is. As best I could hear through my bug--before I got out of range--is that the men are going out to that Redbush place to see if they can find the real estate plat. They don't know which cabin belongs to your dad. Do you?"

"I'm not one-hundred percent certain. My memory is pretty faint on details. I think it's the one with the 'for sale' sign in the front yard. It was ten years ago. There are more trees, more cabins. Nothing looks familiar."

"So, Sam and Rena should be somewhere around here. Maybe they're watching us."

Chelsea lifted herself to a squatting position and peeked around the pine tree. "I don't need to hear that."

"I take it you couldn't get any money."

"No, I don't have it. It'll be a few months before I can touch the money. The estate has to grind through the courts."

"You got a satchel so you can pretend you got it?"

"Well, I could empty the clothes out of my suitcase in the trunk of my car."

"Whew, this is gonna take some careful planning. You should have stayed put and left this job to the professionals."

"I know you're right. Usually after the fact, I always regret my impulsive acts, but I simply couldn't stand the thought of Sam and Rena having Cody." Chelsea continued to peer into the darkness. "I've got enough regrets to last the rest of my life," she mumbled with soft sincerity.

"We're gonna have to do one hell of a bluff job. Damn, I need a cigarette."

Chelsea suddenly placed her hand over Terry's mouth. "Shush," she whispered hoarsely. "It's Sam. He's going into the cabin."

Terry rose to her feet with her back hugging the broad

214

trunk of the tree, then peered sideways toward the group of cabins. "Super, that's our quarry. I'll bet Rena and the baby are already inside. Sam probably went to hide his car."

"According to Mandy, he's driving Daddy's old Rolls Royce. Oh Lord, I could have run smack into him," Chelsea said in a quivering voice as she sank back to the ground. "I'm so green at this detective stuff. If you'll tell me what to do, I'll do it."

"Great. You're a team player. I think I gotta workable plan up my sleeve. Can you cry on demand?" Terry pinched one of Chelsea's cheeks. "I'm talking ear-piercing loud and with complete, uninhibited hysteria."

"It won't take much acting on my part."

***

The threat of rain passed, the clouds cleared and the moon, revealing her true brilliance, illuminated the night. After Sam had entered the cabin, there had been a flurry of activity, followed by the delicious aroma of a cooking pizza. Later, Sam stepped outside the front door to smoke a couple of cigarettes, his lanky body outlined by an oblong shaft of yellow light. After that-- nothing.

"I'm so exhausted. Can't remember the last time I slept." *Certainly not on the previous night,* she thought wryly. She had only catnapped between bouts of wild, uninhibited sex. Chelsea yawned and rubbed her gritty eyes. "We haven't heard a peep or seen one bit of activity for nearly two hours. And I haven't heard Cody cry. Maybe he's not even in the cabin. What should we do?"

"I was sort of hoping they'd take a nap or doze off. Then we can sneak inside the cabin and snatch the baby. If Sam spots us and pulls his gun, well...." Terry confidently readied her pistol with a noisy click releasing the safety latch. "If it's me or him, he loses."

"How long do you think before Logan and the police show up?" Chelsea asked.

"Now that's a good question. I sort of got a feeling that they'll want to ambush before daylight. I know Brew Wilder, and he plays by the book." Terry pushed a tiny button on the side of her man-sized wristwatch to illuminate the face. "It's almost four. I think we should make our move now. You ready?"

"Ready as I'll ever be." Chelsea gripped Terry's shoulder and spoke with controlled desperation. "I've got to protect Cody. No matter what, I've got to make sure we get him out unharmed."

"Girl, maybe we come from different worlds, different generations and we've only known each other a couple of hours, but we got one thing in common--motherhood. I would have killed or laid down my life to protect one of my babies and I'll do the same for yours."

"Why would you put your life in jeopardy for Cody?"

"Let's just say I got a soft spot in my heart for babies. Anybody's baby. Now, gimme the layout of the cabin."

"There are two bedrooms with a bath between on each

side of the house. In the middle is a living room, dining room and kitchen combination stretching the entire length. As I recall there's doors at opposite ends. I haven't seen any lights on in the east-facing bedrooms, so they must be on the other side." After the two women clasped hands, Chelsea drew in a calming breath of air. "Let's go get my son."

From their hidden vantage point, Chelsea and Terry could see only the East side and a small portion of the front of the building. They decided to swing around and approach from the West. The kitchen light was on, and the back door was hanging open.

"Would they be asleep in the bedrooms with the lights on and the back door ajar?" Chelsea querried in a whisper. She was sweating profusely, her bra and blouse were soaked. "And why is the air conditioning turned off?"

"Something doesn't seem right, does it? Come on, stay close to me." Terry motioned for Chelsea to follow as she hesitantly entered the back door. She knew that murderers routinely turned off heat or air conditioning to foul a coroner's attempt to pinpoint time of death, but kept that tidbit of knowledge to herself. The center portion of the house was vacant. Empty beer cans, a half-eaten pizza and opened jars of baby food cluttered the kitchen counter.

The fear, which had been Chelsea's constant companion over the past week, now blossomed into full-blown terror as they tiptoed toward the bedroom. Her nerves were stretched taut and it wouldn't take much to make them snap. A sliver of dim light glowed beneath a partially opened door. The noxious odor struck a primal chord and Chelsea's first instinct was to run as fast and as far as she could, but the overwhelming need to find Cody kept her feet firmly planted.

Where's Cody? The question kept thrashing in her mind with every step, every breath, and every beat of her heart. *Where's my baby?*

There was a soft squeak of hinges as Terry, with gun raised and readied in a two-fisted grip, pushed the door open with her foot. As the two women eased forward, they saw him.

Sam Wheeler lay on his back in the middle of the rumpled bed linens, his clouded eyes staring blankly at the ceiling, a horrified look frozen on his features, and his jaw was locked open in an unuttered scream. The fingers of his right hand were forever clenched around the butt of a revolver still securely tucked in the waistband of his jeans. His left hand dangled over the side of the bed, his fingertips blackened with pooled blood. His shirt had been thrown across the foot of the bed. Light from the weak-watted bedside lamp glistened on the handle of the jewel-encrusted letter-opener buried to the hilt in his chest. Blood had run down both sides of his bare chest forming a slick puddle on the sheet and dripping down to create a crimson stain on the carpet. In the intense heat, Sam's face had become blotchy and discolored, but was still recognizable. Flies had gathered on the thick pink froth in his nose, their soft buzzing audible above the night sounds. The stench arose from his death-released bowels.

Chelsea's scream pierced the quiet of the night.

Chapter 17
Thursday Dawn
Arkabutler, Mississippi

The first bluish-pink hint of dawn was ruthlessly swallowed by morning fog as Chelsea ran from the horror contained within the cabin. Her lungs were desperate in their hunger for oxygen. The scream she thought was rending the countryside, was heard only in the confines of her brain. There was no destination in her thoughts, only to put as much distance as possible between herself and death. Had Cody been a witness to the grisly murder? Would the memory of his abduction scar his young mind? Or would the resiliency of his tender youth protect him?

Where was Cody? Where was Rena?

Wildly arcing beams of light pierced the morning haze. Harsh male voices possessed a strange hollowness as they yelled terse orders. Intuition told her they rang of authority. Help. She was not alone.

The first shot rang out in the stillness and the sound seemed to ricochet repeatedly against the trunks of the stately loblolly pine, ravaging the silent innocence of dawn. A second shot was followed by the thin wail of a child. That tiny whimper soared above all other noise and cut into Chelsea's consciousness.

"Cody!" The underbrush tore mercilessly at her arms and

clothing as she changed directions toward the solitary sound that instinct pulled her. She fought the owner of rough hands that materialized from nowhere and jerked her to an instant standstill. Her neck whiplashed and a million pinpoints of light exploded within her head, threatening her thinly held awareness.

A dozen flashlights crisscrossed the area, finally alighting on the figures of a man and a woman. "Logan? Logan?" Chelsea screamed aloud and finally yanked loose from the deputy who was trying vainly to restrain her. She ran to Logan who was lying face down on the leaf-littered soil. She dropped to her knees. "Logan, say something! Are you all right? Oh God, blood! Where's Cody?" She followed the child's muffled cries on hands and knees. Her baby was lying beneath Rena. She rolled the woman on her back and pulled the screaming child into her arms. Her hands hurriedly searched for injuries and found none. Brew was on her heels and once Chelsea was assured her baby was unhurt, she handed Cody to him and immediately turned her attention back to Logan. "Oh, Lord, please, please don't let Logan die." Finding strength from within, she rolled him over and her fingers began to search for the hidden source of the blood.

Had he not been in so much pain, Logan might have enjoyed the sensations. "My leg," he whispered hoarsely as he looked up at her. "I think I took a hit in my leg."

"Oh, Logan. Thank God you're all right." A plea for forgiveness died on her lips as Logan fainted. She looked up to

221

Brewster Wilder. "We've got to get help."

"I've called for a helicopter, but we've got to get him to an open field."

"We've got to stop the bleeding."

"We don't have any paramedics here. I'll get one of the State Troopers."

"No, I can do it. Give me your tie," Chelsea ordered. She aligned Logan's body, then applied pressure to a tourniquet until the pace of the blood loss slowed. "I refuse to let you die, Logan," she said in a gruff voice. "Do you hear me? You're not going to die."

***

The long hours spent in the hospital waiting room for Logan to emerge from surgery seemed interminable. She paced, drank coffee and tried to carry on a conversation with Tom Guthrie and Sharon Wilder, Logan's mother, but couldn't seem to find any coherent words to exchange with either person. They amused themselves with Cody, while his distracted mother continued to circle the width and breadth of the room.

Chelsea relived those last few hours at Arkabutler in excruciating detail--meeting Terry Hodges, finding Sam's body, the terror of hearing gunshots, Logan's injury, the relief at finding Cody unhurt and the godawful feeling of total abandonment when the helicopter took off with Logan and she was forced to use ground transportation with Tom and Brew. Chelsea felt certain that those images would haunt her dreams for a long time.

Finally, the nurse appeared at the door. "Mister Wilder is out of recovery and you can see him now, if you'd like."

"If I'd like," Chelsea muttered. "Of course, I want to see him now."

"We'll give you thirty minutes."

"Thank you," she mumbled. Her sandals clattered along the hard floor of the hospital as Chelsea hurried down the hall behind the nurse's purposeful stride.

The doctor was standing at the foot of Logan's bed writing on a chart and looked up with a smile as Chelsea entered the room. "Mister Wilder is doing great. He lost a lot of blood when the bullet shattered the femur, but we managed to patch it together with a steel plate. It'll take a while, but I think he'll make a complete recovery. He's still coming out of the anesthesia and won't be fully awake for another hour or so. I'll be back later tonight to check on him."

In Chelsea's eyes, "complete recovery" was a grand overstatement. Logan looked so pale and ill with half a dozen tubes attached to his various body parts. She silently approached. All the words and feelings that she had kept bottled over the past two years came spilling out in a whispered torrent.

"I should have told you, Logan. How can you ever forgive me? It was such a lonely ordeal, the morning sickness, that precious first time I felt our baby move, giving birth alone. For me, it was love at first sight, well, almost. I guess it was when you were talking about 'good guys,' and the earth moving." Her fingers skittered along the surface of his arm. "Oh, Logan, I love you so much. In my selfishness, I wanted you to love me, for me as a person, not because I'm the mother of your son. I've probably ruined everything by telling you so many lies. One piled on top of the other until I knew they would eventually bury me. And they did." Chelsea continued to ramble on for several more agonizing minutes as tears started to fall. "I'll probably spend the rest of my days doing penance."

The nurse tapped on the door. "Kiss him goodbye," she ordered. "Your thirty minutes are up."

Chelsea stopped to catch her breath, then leaned over to place a light kiss on Logan's pale lips. In a flash of movement she thought impossible from his seemingly inert body, Logan grabbed her wrist in a powerful grip. Pulled off balance, she fell on top of him.

"Go back to that part where you said 'I love you so much,'" he whispered hoarsely.

"Logan! You're conscious! You're impossible. How much have you heard?"

"Every word. And I want to hear it again and again. But first, kiss me."

Their lips met in a joyous celebration of life. They were lost in their own private world until Tom Guthrie and Sharon

Wilder stepped into the room and Tom blew out a forced, embarrassed cough. Even though his days of breathless passion had come and gone, he could still recognize the aura of intimacy flowing between them. A flicker of that never forgotten memory of the love he shared with Emily could still bring a smile to his lips. "I was young once," he whispered gruffly.

"Tom, do you remember that lecture you always deliver before every holiday?" Logan asked.

"Huh? Oh yes, you mean about finding a wife?"

"Yeah." Logan lifted Chelsea's chin and looked into those gorgeous violet eyes. "I just found her."

"I also found someone," Sharon said as she stepped into the small room. "Would you like to meet my newest grandson, Cody?"

Logan struggled to lift himself into a sitting position as his dark brown eyes sought the small child.

Chelsea extracted the boy from Sharon's arms and stepped beside Logan's bed. "Cody, this is your daddy."

Epilogue
Christmas Holiday
Memphis, Tennessee

Chelsea Hollander Wilder slipped into jeans and a warm sweater. She had been planning this Christmas surprise for Logan for the last two months and she wouldn't let a little bit of early morning nausea spoil her fun.

Life had come full circle. Nothing would bring back her father, but Chelsea had learned to absolve herself of guilt. Sam Wheeler was dead. Rena Allen Wheeler recovered from her bullet wound and was in jail awaiting trial. She was charged with bigamy, kidnapping, accessory to murder, and second-degree murder. The tox screen indicated that Rena was also guilty of dosing her elderly husband with drugs to induce mental confusion. Rena was fighting the charge of Sam's murder with a defense of spousal abuse. In time, Chelsea knew the loose ends would be tied up and Rena would finally pay for her crimes.

Terry Hodges was another bright spot on the horizon. Ignoring the lure of money, she had not sold the story to anyone. In fact, Terry had become a dear friend, often coming to dinner and amusing everyone with stories of her exploits as a private investigator and part time writer for the supermarket tabloids.

Chelsea felt certain that Claude Hollander would be happy over the way his daughter was handling his estate. Redbush had been sold to a land developer. Much of the ready cash had been spent by Sam and Rena; part Chelsea had given to charity; some to Walter and Doralee. Although Chelsea bought Logan's Christmas present, two new cars and some much-needed furniture, the remainder had been put in an educational trust fund for Cody and the other children that she and Logan would have. Logan was adamant about wanting to support his family without Hollander money.

Doralee was working for Tom Guthrie. Along with Walter and her children, Doralee lived in the roomy apartment over the garage. Tom was like a new man with his bionic knee and a renewed zest for life. Chelsea, Logan and Cody were living in the house at Seventeen Eleven Central Avenue, but that would soon be put up for sale as well. The surprise for Logan was where they would be moving.

"Good morning, Susan." Chelsea beamed as she entered the law offices. "Is my husband back from court?"

"Yes, ma'am."

"Where's Cody?" Logan asked after a welcoming kiss.

"I left him with Doralee. She's doing such a good job looking after Cody and Tom. That old man has turned into a real pussycat over kids. Come on, I've got a surprise for you. Call it an early Christmas present."

"Do I have to close my eyes?"

"Yes, you do."

***

As the wheels of her new red Jaguar crunched over the gravel drive, Chelsea handed her husband a legal document. It was a deed. "You can open your eyes now."

"You bought it? The farm where I grew up?"

They emerged from the car and headed for the front door. Chelsea grasped one of his hands, pressed a key into his palm and rolled his fingers into a fist. "I hope you're not angry over my extravagance?"

"A little bit, but I'm also speechless."

"Do you remember that day last June when you brought me out here the first time?"

"Vividly."

"Do you remember when we walked upstairs and talked about having kids to fill up the bedrooms?"

"I remember that vividly as well."

"I guess we'd better get busy tearing out walls. We're going to be filling the second of those four bedrooms."

"I thought I'd noticed some subtle changes in your body, my darling. I probably knew before you did." Logan gathered her into his arms and kissed her. When his lips covered hers, the December chill, and the outside world ceased to exist.

It was the sixth month into forever.